Blame It On The Eggnog

Samantha Baca

Sugarplum Falls Series

Blame It On The Mistletoe

Blame It On The Eggnog

Blame It On The Candy Canes

Blame It On The Reindeer

Blame It On The Carols

Blame It On The Blizzard

Contents

<u>One</u>
Sunny

"You're late," growled the six-foot-tall beast with piercing blue eyes and brown hair that was glaring at me.

Normally, I would have found him attractive with his broad shoulders and defined jawline, but his attitude alone was enough to turn me off.

"Sorry, there was a reindeer issue on Main Street." I hung my purse on the coat rack behind the door and pulled my scarf from my neck.

"Reindeer?" He arched a perfectly groomed eyebrow.

"Yeah, there was a carrot fiasco, and one of the reindeer got loose. It was a big mess and blocked all lanes of traffic, hence my delay."

"You've got to be kidding," he mumbled, pushing a strong hand through his neatly trimmed hair.

Elliott Weston was new to Sugarplum Falls and was currently the talk of the town, which was huge given that Christmas was in full force. One thing Sugarplum Falls prided itself on was its Christmas spirit, and that showed with how much the town decorated. I wasn't going to be the town's rat, but Elliott was soon going to go from being talked about because he was so good-looking to being talked about because he didn't have a single decoration up—inside or outside. That was basically a sin in Sugarplum Falls.

"So," I started, hoping to change the subject. "Your email said you're looking for help with Alex five days a week. It also mentioned that you might have an occasional weekend where you would need me to watch him as well."

"Yes," he replied, walking briskly to the kitchen and leaving me to follow. "My job keeps me rather busy, however, I work from home, so I'm looking for someone who can take care of Alex while keeping the noise level to a minimum. If that means that you need to take him out of the house during my meetings, then so be it. I will handle any expenses that are incurred from those outings."

"Okay," I said, sitting down in the chair he pulled out before taking one at the other end of the long wooden table. "I understand that he's three, and according to my notes, he's not enrolled in preschool, correct?"

I looked up at him to find his eyes locked on me. I nervously tucked a strand of hair behind my ear and tried not to appear taken aback. I was basically the town's nanny but had never met a parent who intimidated me as much as Elliott did.

"No, he's not in preschool."

I pulled my lips into a thin line and was about to look back at the notes I'd written on the email I printed out when Alex came running into the kitchen.

"Can we play Legos?" he asked, yanking on the sleeve

of Elliott's shirt that wrapped snugly around his bicep. I noticed a hint of tribal ink and looked away as he turned and picked the boy up to set him on the table.

"I'm talking with Sunny right now, but we can play when I'm done."

Alex turned and looked at me, cuddling into his dad's chest as he noticed the stranger in the kitchen.

"Can you say hi? Sunny is going to be your new nanny."

I smiled warmly, hoping to show him that I was nice.

"But I want Magda," Alex pouted and tucked his head into Elliott's chest again.

"Magda was his nanny in Florida."

I nodded but said nothing.

"Why don't you go watch your movie, and I'll come get you when we're done?"

He set Alex back on the floor and patted his back before the boy ran off to the living room.

It was a large, spacious house with beautiful marble floors and brand-new appliances in the kitchen. I hadn't seen the rest of the house yet, but I imagined it was just as gorgeous.

Once we were alone again, Elliott went back into business mode. He went over his schedule and his expectations while I rushed to jot everything down. I was used to working as a nanny for several different families at one time and only as needed.

If I took this job, I would be working exclusively for him,

which meant we would be spending a lot of time together. I wasn't sure if I was ready for such a big step, but I shook his hand and agreed to be there bright and early tomorrow morning anyway.

Two
Elliott

When I picked Sunny to interview as the new nanny for Alex, I pictured an older woman with wrinkled skin who moved slowly and baked fresh chocolate chip cookies. I didn't expect a young, busty blond with curves and legs for days. But after checking her resume, I realized Sunny graduated high school five years ago, which made her twenty-two or twenty-three, unless she was some child genius who graduated early.

I tried to stay professional and focus on the task at hand, but her dark blonde locks had me transfixed on her lips which were painted a light pink glossy color. They were full and pouty and begged to be kissed. Not that I would kiss her—she was far too young for me, and I was hiring her to take care of my son, not me.

Though I really wanted to play with her.

I played Legos with Alex for an hour before cleaning up and starting dinner. We had been in Sugarplum Falls for two weeks, and it felt like I was still trying to find stuff around the house. I rushed to get us unpacked, but that also meant that I didn't remember where half of it went.

Finally, I found the spices that I was looking for and got started.

Alex was sitting at the kitchen table, coloring while I cooked. I loved the time I got with him, but lately, it felt like it was less and less. Work was getting busier, and soon, I would be working overtime again.

It was four weeks until Christmas, and our sales started booming right after Thanksgiving. Who knew that sex toys were the go-to gift for that special loved one? But every year, our reports showed the same spikes during Christmas, Valentine's Day, and Mother's Day.

I turned on the radio mounted beneath one of the cabinets and found a station playing Christmas music. This year was going to be rough for Alex with so many changes, but I prayed that he was young and resilient enough to handle it without much pushback.

His mother and I had been separated for two years—pretty much right after his first birthday. She'd been gone since and hadn't bothered to see him once. He didn't remember much about her, but I still kept a few pictures of them together hung in his room so he could see her if he wanted to. While I couldn't stand the woman, she was still his mother. I owed it to him to give him a chance to know who she was if he wanted to.

When we finally filed for divorce last month, I was furious that she demanded custody of Alex unless I gave her the house in Florida. I knew she didn't want to be a mother and was just using him to get what she wanted, which made me hate her even more. Children should never be used as bargaining chips.

But when it came down to the nitty gritty, I agreed to give her the property in Florida, as well as the yacht, the BMW, and the dog. In exchange, I got full custody of Alex. At the end of the day, I would give up every penny I had to my name if it meant that I had my son.

I turned the stove off and moved the skillet from the burner.

"Alright, Buddy, it's time for dinner. Clean up your mess and go wash your hands."

"Okay, Daddy!" He jumped up and collected his crayons before putting them back in the box.

He was a great kid, and I loved that I didn't have to fight with him to do the stuff I asked him to do.

I scooped some hotdogs and potatoes onto his plate, added some ketchup, and then set it on the table while he washed his hands. I could hear him singing while the water ran and laughed. How could anyone *not* want to be around this cool little dude?

He came out a few minutes later and joined me at the table. We bowed our heads, said a prayer, and then started eating.

"So, what did you think of Sunny?" I asked.

He shrugged and pierced a piece of hotdog with his fork.

"She seems nice, doesn't she?" I pressed, hoping that he would be open to having a new nanny.

He shrugged again and kept eating.

I knew it would be difficult for him not to have Magda around. Hell, if I could have gotten her in the divorce, I would have asked. He was closer to her than anyone else, and it broke my heart when I told him we were moving.

There was nothing keeping us in Florida. In fact, it was the hurricanes and his mother that pushed me as far from there as possible. When I looked into safe places to raise children, an article came up about Sugarplum Falls, Idaho. Not only was it hundreds of miles away from my ex-wife, Sharon, but it was also close to the company that manufactured our products which meant that I could pop in and check on things as needed.

I single handedly started Dark Vibes when I was twenty-two and turned it into the multi-billion-dollar company it is today after fifteen years of hard work and dedication. When people ask why I decided to start a sex toy company, I smile and tell them that I've always known what women want. That's why 90% of our products are designed for them. Men are easy to please; women, on the other hand, deserve more attention.

Alex and I finished up dinner, and then I read him a story and put him to bed. I was having a hard time winding down for the night when I knew Sunny would be showing up at my door first thing in the morning. I tried to keep reminding myself that she was just coming to do a job and scolded my cock for getting so excited.

Three
Sunny

I arrived a few minutes early, nervous to start my first day.

The door opened, and Elliott stood on the other side wearing jeans and a tight-fitting polo, looking absolutely delicious.

"Good morning," I said, stepping inside as he held the door open for me.

"Morning."

The nerves that I felt before I saw him were now magnified to DEFCON 1.

"Alex is still sleeping. He should be up soon."

"Okay," I said, reminding myself that I had done this a thousand times and right now wasn't any different. "I'll look over our notes about his daily routine; however, if there's anything specific you'd like me to handle first, please let me know. If not, I'll wait for him to get up, and then we'll get the day started."

"Go ahead and let him sleep however long he wants to. He's good about taking care of using the bathroom on his own when he wakes up, but sometimes he needs a gentle reminder."

"Got it. Is there anything you'd like me to fix him for breakfast?"

"I went grocery shopping yesterday, so the fridge is fully stocked. Help yourself to whatever you'd like. As far as Alex, he can be a picky eater in the morning, so I usually let him tell me what he wants."

"Sounds good. Would you like me to fix anything for you?"

His brow furrowed for a brief moment.

"No, that's not necessary. Your job is to take care of Alex, not tend to me."

I raised an eyebrow in irritation.

"You may not be used to small cities, Mr. Weston, but it's just common courtesy to offer food to everyone in the house—whether it's *your job* or not. It's called being a decent human being."

Elliott opened his mouth to speak but was interrupted by Alex walking down the hallway, rubbing his eyes sleepily.

"Hey, good morning, Buddy. How did you sleep?"

He knelt in front of him, getting to his eye level.

"Good."

"I have to start my day, but Sunny is going to hang out with you and make some breakfast. Just let her know what you want, okay?"

Alex nodded and looked up at me, unsure whether to trust me, as Elliott ruffled his hair and then walked down the hall to his office.

Once I heard the door close, I squatted in front of him and held out my hand.

"We haven't officially met," I said. "I'm Sunny."

His small hand fell lightly into mine as he shook it. It felt weird to be introduced to a kid like this, but their situation was different. When I would nanny for someone in town, it was always families that I already knew and children that I was familiar with. I hadn't had a child who didn't know me before, and I was worried that Alex would take a long time to open up to me.

"I'm Alex."

"I've heard a lot about you, but I'm sure you're curious about me. So, why don't we get you ready for the day, and you can ask me any questions you have. We'll be spending a lot of time together, so I want you to feel comfortable around me."

He nodded and pulled his hand back.

"Alright, first things first," I said, standing up and walking with him down the hallway to the bathroom. I smiled when he noticed the Converse shoes I was wearing, his little blue eyes staring at them in amazement. They were plain white when I bought them, but I'd painted different characters on them over the past few months and wore them whenever I was nannying. I had a few pairs that I'd done this with and took a chance on wearing my superhero ones today, hoping they would have characters that Alex might recognize.

I waited outside the bathroom while he closed the door and took care of his business. Once he was done, I had him give me a tour of the house. While I could have asked Elliott to show me around, I found that it built a better bond with the kids if I allowed them to show me. It gave them a sense of pride to show off what was important to them and made them feel included in what we were doing.

We headed into the kitchen, and I opened the fridge, scanning the contents to see what we were working with.

"What would you like for breakfast?" I asked, peeking around the door to look at him.

"Pancakes with the little sprinkles in them."

"Sprinkles?"

He nodded.

This wasn't my first rodeo, and Elliott had already warned me that Alex could be a picky eater. I closed the door and joined him at the table.

"That sounds fun. Can you tell me more about them?"

His eyes lit up as he went into great detail about the pancakes. Apparently, they were special pancakes that his other nanny used to make him. I asked as many questions as possible until I felt confident I could recreate what he was asking for.

I searched through the cabinets, hoping to find what I needed but came up empty handed. I hated the disappointed look on Alex's face when I broke it to him that there were no sprinkles. I was feeling defeated until I found a bag of chocolate chips.

"Have you ever had chocolate smiley face pancakes?" I asked, shaking the bag in front of me.

He shook his head but didn't have the enthusiasm I hoped for.

"Would you like to try some?"

"Okay," he sighed with a shrug.

I opened the box of pancake mix and got started. I checked on Alex several times as he sat at the kitchen table and watched me. I offered for him to come help, but he declined. He needed time to get used to me, so I didn't take it personally. It was a big step for him to try something new with the smiley face pancakes, so I wasn't going to press my luck.

Once they were done, I plated one and set it in front of him, waiting for his reaction.

He looked at them and then smiled.

I sighed a breath of relief and sat down while he ate.

The day might've started a little shaky, but I was confident it would get better.

Four
Elliott

"What do you mean the vibrator isn't vibrating? That's literally its only job," I muttered into the phone, annoyed that our product manager was reporting an issue with a new toy we were launching this week.

I pinched the bridge of my nose and tried to ignore the throbbing headache that was forcing its way over my eyes.

"I don't care whose fault it is," I snapped. "Get it fixed. Now."

I hung up the phone and leaned back in the high-back ergonomic office chair that my last assistant insisted that I purchase for my constant back pain. I was only thirty-seven, but apparently, that was old enough to worry about which chairs would kill my back and which would help.

I looked down at the clock on my computer and noticed it was almost lunchtime. I marked myself as out of the office in the system so all calls would be forwarded directly to my voicemail. When I joined Alex for lunch, I made sure that I was present and not distracted by anything happening in my office.

It had been quiet most of the morning, so I was curious about what Sunny and Alex had been up to. I'd given her permission to take him out of the house if needed but hoped she would at least give me a heads-up if she decided to. I'd given her my phone number and asked that she text me if she needed to reach me.

As I rounded the corner into the kitchen, I found Sunny at the stove and Alex sitting at the kitchen table.

"What's your favorite color?" he asked.

"Red," she answered, looking over her shoulder to engage him. "What's yours?"

"Blue."

"That was my dad's favorite color."

"Does he still like blue?"

She stilled for a second and then flipped the sandwich in the pan before answering.

"He's not here anymore."

She didn't say any more, and luckily, Alex didn't push for more information.

"What's going on in here?" I asked, leaning against the door frame with my arms folded.

"Daddy!" Alex hopped down from his chair and wrapped his little arms around my waist.

I bent down and picked him up, giving him the tightest squeeze I could without hurting him.

"Hey, Buddy!"

"Sunny is making grilled cheese!"

"She is?"

I smiled at him, loving the way his face lit up for the first time in the weeks we'd been here.

"Would you like one?" Sunny offered, glancing at me over her shoulder.

I was about to tell her that I could make my own lunch but then remembered the stern comment she had made earlier about small towns and making enough food for everyone.

"Umm, sure. That would be great. Thank you."

I joined her by the stove while Alex hopped back up on the chair he was sitting on.

"Can I help with anything?"

Sunny reached around me to grab a plate, and I felt her breasts brush against my arm. She seemed to notice the spark as quickly as I did because she pulled back and her cheeks reddened.

"If you want to get the veggies out of the fridge and wash them, that would be great. We need the carrots and celery."

"Got it."

I kept myself busy while Sunny worked on the sandwiches. Once the veggies were washed, she showed me how she wanted them cut and guided me on adding peanut butter down the middle of each slice of celery.

She cut the tips of the carrots off into thin slices and placed them at one end of the celery, then added a twisted pretzel that she broke in half to the other end to make antlers. I was already starting to see the reindeer, but the final touch was when she opened a small can of sliced olives and cut them into small pieces to make eyes.

Alex was excited when she set his plate down. He loved the reindeer so much that I couldn't remember the last time I saw him eat veggies that fast.

I took a bite of my sandwich and continued to watch my son, already in awe of the progress that Sunny was making without even knowing.

I leaned over and whispered so only she could hear.

"Good job getting him to eat vegetables. Very creative."

"Thanks. I have a few tricks up my sleeve." She took a bite of her reindeer and then licked the peanut butter from the side of her mouth.

I felt my dick hardening and looked away. Now wasn't the time or place for that, especially with my kid sitting right there. Though I definitely wondered what other *tricks* she might have.

"Do you have any pets?" Alex asked around a mouthful of grilled cheese.

I frowned in confusion, wondering where that came from. It was totally random and unlike Alex to talk with his mouth full.

Sunny swallowed her bite and then wiped her mouth before answering.

"In an effort for Alex to get to know me, he can ask questions as they come to him," she explained before turning to him. "I don't have any right now, but I used to have a pet rabbit named Fluffy when I was a little girl."

"What color was it?"

"White."

"Was it fluffy?"

She scrunched her face and shook her head.

"No," she laughed. "It really wasn't. It was short-haired and kinda mean. It used to steal my socks and hide them. I was always late for school, and my mom never believed me when I said I couldn't find any socks because Fluffy had taken them. Then one day, she caught her in the act, and we found a collection of them stuffed in a corner under my bed where she used to hide."

Alex tipped his head back and laughed. My heart felt like it was going to explode by how much it was swelling with happiness.

I continued eating my lunch, watching them interact as if they were best friends who had known each other forever.

When I asked around town about a nanny, people couldn't stop recommending Sunny. Now I understand why.

Five
Sunny

I absolutely loved spending the day with Alex. He showed me his toys and brought handfuls into the living room so we could play. Their house was big, with plenty of space, and Alex even had a designated playroom that contained most of his stuff. His bedroom was clean and tidy, and I could tell that it was designed only for sleeping.

I was going to suggest that we hang out in the playroom, but when Elliott's angry voice carried through the thin walls as he yelled at someone on the phone, I decided it was better to stay in the living room. Not only did I not want to risk Alex getting too loud and interrupting Elliott, but I also didn't think a three-year-old needed to start asking questions about vibrators. I had no idea what kind of work Elliott did, but I was growing more curious by the minute.

By five o'clock, Elliott was still in his office, and Alex was asking for a snack, so I decided to start dinner. We hadn't talked about whether this was within my scope of what he expected me to do, but I figured if it was okay for me to prepare breakfast and lunch, then it should also be okay to make dinner.

Alex was busy playing in the living room with his superheroes while I kept an eye on him from the kitchen. A few walls technically separated the rooms, but for the most part, it was an open concept that allowed me to see directly to where he was playing from where I was standing.

Elliott's office door opened, and I heard him storm down the hall, his heavy footsteps echoing off the marble floors.

"Sorry I was late tonight. You can go."

I pulled my head back and turned toward him.

"Excuse me?"

"I said you can go."

"Okay. I was in the middle of making dinner…"

"And I said you can go. Your day is over."

I set the spoon that I had stirred the pasta with down on the granite countertop and stepped away. I pressed my lips together to keep from saying something rude or worse—from crying.

It seemed Elliott had several different personalities, and I liked this one the least. He was cold and abrupt, with no warning whatsoever.

"Alright, Alex. I'm going home, but I'll see you in the morning. Okay?"

He got up and came running in to give me a hug as I pulled my coat down from the rack by the door.

"Are you kidding me? What's with the mess?" Elliott's voice boomed, startling both Alex and me.

"He was playing while I cooked. I was going to clean it up as soon as I was done."

He planted his hands on his hips and looked from me to his son.

"We don't bring out that many toys at once. You know that. Once you're done playing with something, you put it away."

"Sorry, Dad."

Alex clung to my side, lowering his head in shame.

"Hey," I snapped, bringing Elliott's attention to me. "It's not his fault. I said he could bring those toys out and play with them."

"Yes, and he knows the rules."

"And obviously, you haven't stopped yelling at people to take the time to tell me about them."

I gently pushed Alex behind me as I stood toe to toe with his father.

"It's common sense, Sunny. Who needs that many toys out at once?"

"A kid, Elliott. One who is having fun and enjoying their childhood."

"They can do that without making a mess."

"Who was it bothering? No one."

"Me! It bothers me!"

His voice boomed through the house, and I felt Alex's hands dig into the fabric of my coat.

"You're scaring your son. Is that what you want?"

"You've been in our lives for one day—don't act like you know anything about us or what we want. I can find another nanny—"

My blood was boiling as I stared into his icy blue eyes, wondering if there was a soul attached to his body or if it was just Satan in disguise.

"No, Daddy!"

Alex jumped out from behind and stood in front of me.

"You can't get rid of Sunny! I like her! You already got rid of Magda. You can't take Sunny too!"

My heart ached at the sadness in his voice which just happened to be the thing that got through to Elliott. Suddenly, his face fell, and the anger that was etched on it seconds ago evaporated into thin air. He dropped to his knees and pulled his son in for a hug, holding him while he cried.

"I'm sorry, Alex. I didn't mean to upset you."

I waited to make sure Alex was okay before I left. I didn't want him any more unhappy than he already was, nor did I want him to worry that he was going to lose me.

"I like Sunny," he cried into his dad's shoulder. "Don't make her leave."

"I won't," he assured, looking up and locking eyes with me. "I promise."

Once Alex was calm, Elliott sent him to the living room to start cleaning up some of the mess but promised he would come help him after he walked me out.

I was more than capable of leaving on my own, but I assumed he wanted to talk about what just happened. Typically, I would mind my manners and be polite if there was a disagreement with a parent, but Elliott Weston was a totally different breed that I wasn't sure how to handle. His temper was as hot as he looked when his eyes locked onto me and held me in place.

Once we were outside, Elliott pulled the door closed behind him.

"I'm sorry about that," he said, rocking on his heels and shoving his hands into his pockets.

"About what? Talking to someone the way you did or upsetting your child who saw it?"

He sighed heavily and then looked up at me with this stupidly adorable guilty grin.

"Both."

I shook my head and looked away, frustrated with my uterus for being so freaking easily influenced by this. *He just acted like the biggest asshole in the world, and one deep-dimpled grin is going to make you want to rip your panties off for him?* Get. A. Grip.

No—NOT on his cock.

"Thanks for the apology." I ignored the blush creeping up my cheeks at the inappropriate thoughts and hoped he would assume it was just from the blisteringly cold wind that whipped past us. I turned and headed for my car when his hand reached out and stopped me. The heat that spread through the thick layers of fabric through to my skin was intense. I froze, refusing to look at him until I could assure myself that I wouldn't wrap my legs around him and try to ride him into the sunset.

"Sunny, I really am sorry. You didn't deserve to be treated

that way, and I'd hate for us to start on the wrong foot."

Deep breaths… Just keep breathing. If you don't, you're going to pass out. If you pass out, he's going to have to do CPR.

I let out an awkwardly shaky breath after realizing that I might've been holding it a little too long in the hopes that he would have to save me.

"It's fine. I'll see you in the morning."

I didn't allow him to say anything else as I freed my arm from his grip and climbed into the safety of my car. Once inside, I pressed the button to lock the doors three times just to keep myself from getting out and jumping on him as he waved goodbye before heading back inside to Alex.

<u>Six</u>
Elliott

Thanks to Alex, I now knew a lot about Sunny. He spent last night at dinner telling me what all he'd learned yesterday, from the kind of music she listened to, what types of food she liked, her favorite candy, and that Christmas was her favorite holiday because it felt magical. I couldn't remember the last time I heard him talk so much and had to stop and guess what a few words were because he was confusing them with other ones.

He was a fast learner, and by the time his third birthday rolled around, I joked that he would be getting in trouble in school for being the Chatty Kathy. Over the past month, Alex had less and less to say, and I worried that he was withdrawing to the point of being one of those kids who never talked. Apparently, all he needed was a fun, loveable nanny named Sunny to change all of that for him.

After I got Alex to bed, I spent a few hours talking to the production manager who had an update on the vibrator. Thankfully, the other manufacturer we used quickly identified the issue and corrected the wiring that was keeping it from working properly. Everyone would be working overtime to fix the thousands of units that needed it, but this was already projected to be one of our top sellers this year, so we couldn't afford to not get it out on time.

This morning, I woke up earlier than normal and decided to try to make a better impression on Sunny. I knew that yesterday had been a rough start and was thankful that she hadn't flipped me the bird and stormed out. I could tell that the only reason she stuck around was to make sure Alex was okay, and that was fine with me. After all, he was the most important thing right now, and I did hire her to make sure he had only the best.

Besides, what was I going to do without Sunny anyway? Everyone in town raved about how wonderful she was when I first moved here, and I'd gone to great lengths with doubling her asking rate to get her to agree to be exclusive to Alex. I knew that she bounced around with other families as needed, but I was willing to pay extra for the convenience of not having to shuffle him around between different sitters and a nanny.

Alex was still sleeping when Sunny arrived. She said good morning and hung her coat and purse up before heading into the kitchen. I'd already started a pot of coffee, and thanks to Alex, I knew she preferred hazelnut creamer and two sugars—which I just so happened to have ready for her next to the only Christmas-looking mug I owned. It was red—that was it. But it was the best I could do.

"How was your evening?" I asked, sipping my coffee and trying desperately to engage her in conversation this morning.

"Fine."

"I made coffee."

She glanced at the pot, and then her eyes sparkled for a few seconds when she noticed the creamer, but it faded as quickly as it appeared.

"Good for you."

Ouch. Okay, I deserved that. I'd been a dick to her yesterday and she wasn't going to let me off the hook that easily.

"I made some for you," I offered, lifting my cup in the direction, just in case she missed it—which she didn't.

"Thank you."

This wasn't going well at all. I felt stupid for wishing that Alex would wake up and help me through this awkward interaction with Sunny.

Suddenly, she spun around and grabbed her keys from her purse before darting out the door.

I set my cup down and followed after her.

"What's wrong?"

She was bent over, digging around in the trunk of her car, which put her ass on display in the tight jeans she was wearing.

"Nothing. I forgot I went to the store last night to get stuff for Alex."

I frowned as she breezed past me and set the bags down on the island.

"If he needs stuff, just let me know, and I'll get it. I don't expect you to pay for things he needs."

She held her hand up to silence me.

"It's fine. It's stuff that I wanted to buy."

She began unpacking the bags, and I found myself curiously standing on my tiptoes to see what was inside.

"What did you get?"

"Stuff," she replied, setting the stuff behind the bag so I couldn't see it.

"You're really not going to tell me?"

She stopped and lifted her head, pulling her shoulders back defiantly.

"It's for Alex. Not you." She smiled, but it wasn't one of those nice, sincere ones. It was wicked, like the women my mom used to warn me to stay away from.

I shook my head, grabbed my coffee, and was about to head to my office when I suddenly remembered that I needed to tell her something.

"Hey, before I forget, a woman is coming around two this afternoon to decorate for Christmas. If you could let her in, that would be great. She knows what needs to be done and should bring everything she needs, but if she gets to be a bother, just text me and let me know."

She stopped what she was doing and stared at me. I couldn't read the expression on her face, but I sure as hell knew that I didn't want to see it ever again.

"You've hired someone to come in and decorate your house for you?"

"Yes."

"Why?"

"Because I don't have time to do it, and in case you haven't noticed, this town is kinda obsessed about Christmas."

She shook her head and rolled her eyes.

"What? What's the problem?" I asked, feeling my irritation quickly grow again.

"You really don't get it, do you?"

Her hand was planted firmly on her hip.

"Get what?"

"Instead of hiring someone to come decorate for you, you should be taking the time to decorate with Alex."

My shoulders fell along with my heart.

"It may not mean much to you, but you have no idea how much it will mean to him. How excited he'll be to help you and how every time he looks at the decorations you guys put up, he'll feel proud that he did it. He's still young, but he's making memories, and you should at least be present for them."

She gave me one last disgusted look and then walked down the hallway to greet Alex, who was calling for her from his bedroom.

I blew out a frustrated breath and went to my office, slamming my door behind me.

Seven
Sunny

Alex and I were sitting on the couch watching one of the cartoons he loved when the doorbell rang. I hadn't seen much of Elliott, other than the thirty-minute lunch he took where he shoved a peanut butter and jelly sandwich into his mouth and mumbled a few words to his son before heading back to the office.

I still felt irritated about our conversation this morning, but it would be out of line for me to talk to him about it. What he did in his personal life was none of my business. The best I could do was hope that, at some point, he slowed down and spent the time with Alex that he needed. Some parents got so busy with their careers that they sacrificed their families for it.

I checked my watch and saw it was two o'clock on the dot. Alex was laughing at the cartoon as I got up and opened the door to the woman who was hired to come decorate. I'd spent the day thinking of ways that I could try to get Alex involved in it without him being in the way, but I kept coming up blank.

When I opened the door, it wasn't a woman standing there but two teenage boys I used to babysit.

"What are you guys doing here?" I asked, opening the door so they could come in and set down the bags that lined each of their arms.

"Making a delivery," Josh said, adjusting his beanie before heading back to the truck to grab some of the boxes from the back. Brad set his bags down and then ran out to help him bring in the rest.

I wasn't sure what was going on, so I told them to leave them in the kitchen and that I would let Elliott know they were there.

Before I could get a text message sent, his office door opened, and he came down the hall with a huge grin on his face.

"Thanks so much, guys. I appreciate your help with this."

They grinned like the little goofballs they were when he tipped them fifty bucks each and sent them on their way.

"What's all that?" I asked, too nosey to mind my manners.

"Decorations."

He started peeking in each bag until he found the one that had what he was looking for.

"I thought you had some woman coming to do it for you?"

"I was, but then someone very wise reminded me that I needed to be more present. So, I canceled that and put in an order at Waldon's. I called and asked if they could deliver, and they said no, but then it turned out that the manager who was working had two sons who would be willing to drop everything off for me."

I felt like my jaw was still hanging on the floor when he stood in front of me, his hands behind his back.

"This is to say I'm sorry for how I've acted."

He held out a coffee mug that was shaped into Rudoph's head and had a bright red ball on the opposite side of the handle.

"This is adorable!" I squealed, taking it from him and examining it. "Thank you. You didn't need to buy me anything."

"I know I didn't need to. I wanted to. I thought you might like your own mug to drink your morning coffee out of while you're here."

"I really appreciate it."

We smiled at each other, but it felt like something had shifted between us. I could tell both of us felt it because we separated as quickly as possible.

"Hey, Buddy, want to come help us decorate the house for Christmas?" Elliott called to Alex.

He was off the couch and in the kitchen within seconds, eagerly going through the bags of stuff with his dad.

I stood back and watched, feeling the fondness in my heart grow.

We worked as a team, setting things on the table and organizing. Once that was done, they stood there, staring, wondering what to do next.

"What?" I laughed nervously. "Why are you guys looking at me like that?"

"I bought the stuff to decorate, but I was hoping you'd have a plan for where to start," Elliott whispered loudly behind his hand, earning a giggle from Alex.

I scanned the room and then found the box with the artificial tree.

"I say we start with the tree, then go from there."

Alex gave Elliott a high five, and then they worked on getting the pieces unpacked from the box while I sat on the floor in the living room and read the directions. It should have been super easy to assemble, but Elliott did nothing the easy way and bought a high-tech tree that required a little more focused attention than I had.

I was still reading the directions when I heard some banging, followed by a loud thump. I looked up to see them standing proudly next to the tree that had been assembled in two seconds flat.

"How the heck did you do that? I haven't even gotten past the first few sentences."

"We're men. We build things." Elliott said in his best caveman voice, which Alex immediately copied as they thumped their fists against their chests a few times.

I tossed the instructions down and got up to help Elliott move it. He cleared a spot by the window while Alex and I talked about what ornaments he wanted to put up first.

I stepped back and let the boys put up the decorations, while I curled my feet under me on the couch. I didn't want to intrude on something so special since they were starting brand new memories together. This was amazing, and I was relieved that Elliott had heard me after all this morning.

They were about halfway through putting the bulbs on the tree when Elliott bent down and whispered something in Alex's ear. His grin spread across his adorable little face, then he ran over, grabbed my hand, and led me over to Elliott.

"We'd love it if you would help us," he said softly, handing me an ornament.

I glanced nervously at Alex and then looked up at Elliott.

"I don't want to overstep. This is something you guys should do together."

I chose my words carefully.

"We are doing it together. But we want you to join us."

I watched as Alex hung a few more, completely oblivious to our conversation.

"I don't want to intrude," I whispered.

"You're not."

I was about to object again when Elliott stepped closer to me and wrapped a hand around my waist. He placed his lips right next to my ear, his warm breath tickling my skin.

"Alex has already taken to you in the two days he's spent with you and likes you better than most people he's known his entire life. *I* like you too. You're not overstepping."

My words were caught in my throat, unable to answer.

He dropped his hand from my waist, gently grazing my ass in the process.

My heart fluttered wildly in my chest while thoughts of what *couldn't* happen blossomed in my mind.

Eight
Elliott

Grazing my hand over Sunny's ass was pure heaven and hell. I wanted to touch her, taste her, hear her soft voice as she moaned my name through her cries of ecstasy. But I couldn't. No matter how much I wanted to, Sunny was off limits, and I couldn't risk messing things up with her because of Alex.

It was fun decorating the tree and the rest of the house with her and Alex, and I found myself grateful that she reminded me to step back and spend the time doing it with him instead of hiring someone. I was so used to throwing money at whatever I wanted that I sometimes forgot about the little things that mattered.

Sunny and Alex laughed and hung the ornaments while I tacked up the strings of lights along the ceiling. It was all great fun until I realized Sunny had grabbed a bag of fake snow that I was pretty sure I hadn't ordered and was opening it.

"What are you doing with that?" I asked, frowning from the top of the ladder.

"I'm going to make it snow," she answered, her face adorably tight with a challenging expression as she took a handful out of the bag and held it in the air in front of her.

My eyes followed the pieces that fell to the floor, knowing

how much of a mess this was going to make.

"Sunny," I warned, quickly making my way down the rungs until my feet were firmly planted on the carpet. "That's going to make a mess."

Her emerald green eyes lit up with delight as she tossed it in the air, watching as it fell on my head and all around me.

"Oooops," she giggled, stepping away when I reached for her.

"Oh, you're going to pay for that," I threatened, reaching out to grab her as she tried to run away.

"Oh yeah, what are you going to do?" Her voice was full of mischief and flirtier than usual, which made me wonder if she was feeling the chemistry between us too.

"You don't want to know."

I grabbed her by the waist and pulled her into me, tickling her sides as she squirmed and tried to get away. The living room was filled with laughter as Alex joined in with trying to tickle her.

"Daddy's gonna spank you," he laughed, sending a jolt right through me when I took it another way than he intended.

Sunny's eyes widened as she pulled her bottom lip between her teeth. She was still locked between my arms as her chest heaved from all of the moving around.

Suddenly, I let go, stepping away from her as I processed what Alex had said. While he meant it innocently, I couldn't get my head to stop thinking about how wonderful it would be to have her bent over my knee while I spanked her bare ass.

"We don't spank," I said awkwardly, more to Alex than Sunny. It was something that we'd been talking about recently after he told me that he overheard Magda talking to someone about how children needed a good spanking every now and then. I'd put a stop to that the second I found out.

Sunny's face flushed with embarrassment as she looked down at the mess on the floor.

"I'm sorry about the snow," she apologized, holding her hands in front of her. "I saw it at the store yesterday while I was getting sprinkles and thought it might be fun."

I pulled my lips into a thin line, unsure what to say.

"Well, we have everything just about decorated, so I'm going to start dinner."

Sunny nodded and helped Alex with the last few ornaments while I went to the kitchen and took a deep breath to bring my blood pressure back down.

I had no idea what I was going to make, so I opened the fridge and grabbed random ingredients while they laughed and told silly knock-knock jokes.

Twenty minutes later, Sunny sent Alex to wash up for dinner while she cleaned up the snow from the carpet. I tried to keep my focus on the food I was cooking, but I was constantly distracted by her and didn't want her to leave, even though her day was technically over now.

When she came into the kitchen, I made a rash decision before thinking it through.

"Hey, would you like to join us for dinner?" I asked,

flipping the hamburger patties in the pan. I'd already made one for her, hoping that she would stay.

Her eyes widened briefly, followed by a confused head tilt.

"Why are you inviting me?"

A deep chuckle escaped my throat, making Sunny study me even more.

"Because I made plenty of food, and it's dinner time." I shrugged.

"Just like it's not my job to feed you, it's not your job to feed me."

"I never said it was," I corrected. "I'm inviting you to stay. It's your choice if you'd rather not. But if you stay, you stay as our guest—not my employee."

She opened her mouth to say something but stopped when Alex rushed in.

"Please stay, Sunny!" He yanked at her hands, hopping in front of her with excitement.

She bent down to his level and smiled a smile that I could look at every single day.

"I would be honored to join you guys for dinner," she said, squeezing his hands gently. "I'll go wash up and then see what your dad needs help with."

Alex was still bouncing around, excited about our guest, so I gave up on trying to get him to focus on clearing the table while Sunny was in the restroom. A few minutes later, she returned and stood next to me in the kitchen.

"What can I help with?" she asked, leaning in close enough as she peered into the skillet that her breasts grazed against my arm.

My raging hard erection that would love to be buried deep inside of you.

"I got it, thanks." I cleared my throat, trying to force the thickness out of it.

"You sure? You seem a *little flushed.*" I felt her press herself tighter against my body and stilled. My cock was straining against my jeans, begging to be free. "I was worried maybe the *heat* was getting to you."

She reached forward and turned the burner down as the grease sizzled and popped in the skillet.

"I wouldn't want you to get burned." She smiled coyly and then walked away, helping Alex get the table set for us.

I turned off the skillet and stepped back, feeling flushed and flustered. It was an easy dinner, but Sunny didn't complain when we sat down to eat burgers and chips. She picked her favorite—which I just happened to know was BBQ flavored, thanks to Alex, and lifted her patty to her mouth, parting her beautifully plump lips as she took my meat inside.

A hamburger, dumbass. Not your meat. Just meat that you cooked. Get a hold of yourself.

We talked about Christmas, and Alex mentioned some new toys he wanted after seeing ads for them on TV. Sunny watched intently as if she was taking a mental note of what he wanted.

Then she turned to me and asked, "What would you like

for Christmas? Are there any toys you've got your heart set on?"

I swallowed hard, my throat instantly dry as I tried to decide how to answer.

"I can't think of anything yet. What about you?"

I was dying to know what kind of toys Sunny liked, but I had to refrain from jumping too far down that rabbit hole while my son was sitting at the table.

"I have a few things on my list that I plan to send to Santa," she said with a huge grin that she shared with Alex.

"I'll be sending Alex's letter to Santa soon. I can send yours too if you'd like," I offered, shifting in the wooden chair as I tried to adjust myself under the table.

"I don't know if I trust you not to read it." She narrowed her eyes playfully at me. "I think I might be in better hands if I drop it off at the mall myself."

I licked my lips, thinking about how she'd be in great hands if I had my way.

The rest of dinner was uneventful, and the conversation was redirected to more Alex-appropriate topics. It was already getting late, and I was going to get Alex ready for bed when he asked if Sunny could read him a story instead.

She looked unsure, but I assured her it was fine and gave them some time while I cleaned up dinner. A little while later, she joined me in the kitchen and leaned against the counter.

"I'm sorry, he fell asleep while I was reading."

"It's okay; that's usually how I get him down for the night."

"I feel bad that you didn't get to say goodnight to him."

"Don't," I said as I finished wiping down the countertop and laid the towel on the edge of the sink. "I get to say goodnight every night. He was excited to have you here tonight."

She fidgeted with the sleeves of her shirt for a second as she avoided looking up at me.

"Thank you for inviting me to stay."

"You're welcome."

The heat that radiated between our bodies was enough to make me want to strip off some clothes or turn the air conditioner on. I desperately wanted to act on this attraction to Sunny but knew that I shouldn't. I couldn't ruin this for Alex.

"I guess I should get going," she said nervously as if she didn't want to go.

"You can stay if you want to."

I don't know why I said that when I knew it would be better for her to go. If she left, she would take the temptation with her, and I would be alone and forced to deal with it by myself in the privacy of my bedroom.

She looked up at me under thick, dark eyelashes.

I could see that she was fighting this as much as I was, and it turned me the fuck on.

Without thinking it through, I shortened the gap between us and wrapped my arm around her waist.

A small gasp escaped her mouth before my lips crashed down over it. I knew I shouldn't do this, but nothing could stop me now.

Her hands wrapped around my neck and tugged at my short hair as I kissed her harder, begging her with my tongue to let me in. She whimpered and opened her mouth, our tongues dancing to a beat only they could hear.

I lifted her, and she wrapped her legs around my waist, no doubt feeling my hard cock pressing against her opening.

We were both panting as I set her down on top of the counter and nudged her head to the side as I slowly kissed the side of her neck.

My hand roamed over her breasts, feeling her nipples harden through the thin fabric of her bra and shirt.

I wanted more, needed more. But before I could be more reckless than I already was, I pulled away and shoved a hand through my hair as she stared at me.

"I'm sorry, we shouldn't be doing this."

She nodded, her face falling in disappointment. I helped her down and then walked her out, neither of us willing to say anything about what just happened.

When she got in her car, she didn't look at me before pulling out of the driveway and leaving. I had tried so hard not to fuck things up between us, but I just crossed a line that I couldn't come back from.

Nine
Sunny

It had been a week since the kiss with Elliott, and I'd tried desperately to forget it. But how do you forget something that felt so perfect that it knocked your socks off? No matter how hard I tried, that kiss would forever be ingrained in my memory while I fantasized about what it might feel like to do more with him.

After our mini make-out session, Elliott spent the rest of the week locked up in his office while I was there. We didn't talk or see each other much, which really drove home his message about it being a mistake.

I knew he was older than me, though I couldn't imagine it was *that much*. When I casually tried to ask Alex how old his dad was, he said he didn't know but that he was alive when the dinosaurs roamed the earth.

Against my better judgment, I had spent a few hours each night Googling Elliott Weston and had found plenty of rabbit holes to dive into.

While I discovered that he was thirty-seven, I also stumbled upon an article about the toy business he owned and operated. It seemed Dark Vibes was a thriving online adult toy company and had been featured in several different stores.

When I read the write-up on Elliott and how he built his empire when he was only twenty-two, I couldn't believe it. He was a beast when it came to business, and I couldn't stop myself from wondering if he was one in the bedroom too. I mean, the guy sold sex toys for a living—how could he possibly be bad at sex? Plus, there was the way he kissed and touched me that hinted that he knew what he was doing.

I got ready, debating on whether to wear my red skirt for a day of playing with Alex and then decided to add some thick leggings underneath it to make sure it was appropriate. Not only was it loose and flowy, but it hugged my curves without feeling too sexy. It was my favorite skirt to wear this time of year, and deep down, I hoped that Elliott would like it too.

When I got to the house, I walked through the door to find Alex crying at the table and Elliott looking frustrated and overwhelmed at the stove.

I quickly took my coat off and hung it beside my purse on the coat rack before heading in to see what the problem was.

"What happened?" I asked, squatting down beside Alex as he turned and wrapped his arms around my neck. His face was wet with tears, and his little body shook as he cried. I shushed quietly as I rubbed his back, working to calm him down while Elliott tossed the towel down behind him.

"He's having a fit over the pancakes," he blew out angrily.

I looked from him to Alex and waited for him to look up at me.

"Hey," I said softly. "I can see that you're upset. Can you tell me what happened?"

I ignored Elliott as he puffed his chest with air and then exhaled heavily.

"They. Don't. Have." He hiccupped in a sob and then kept talking. "Sprinkles!"

I wrapped my arms around him and held him until he stopped crying.

"It's okay," I said warmly. "How about you go wash your face with some cold water, and I'll talk to your dad for a moment? Then I'll make you some pancakes with sprinkles."

He nodded and hopped down from the chair before heading to the bathroom. Once he was gone, I stood up and studied Elliott.

"I can't take these fucking fits," he bit out and shook his head.

"It's not a fit. He's frustrated."

"Over fucking pancakes!" He threw his hands in the air.

I tried to keep myself calm as I spoke and avoided getting as worked up as he was. I needed to be the one who fixed the problem, not make them worse.

"To you, they're just pancakes," I started. "But to him, they're something special."

He arched an eyebrow and waited for me to continue.

"I know it's hard to feel helpless, but Alex isn't trying to make your life harder right now. He's trying to figure out his new normal, and this isn't it."

"What the hell are you talking about?"

"You may not know this, but Magda used to make Alex special pancakes with sprinkles. He told me about it the first day I was here last week. That's why I went to the store that night to get sprinkles. I explained that I knew they were special to him, and I apologized that I couldn't make them that day because I didn't have everything I needed. But to him, Elliott, they're not just pancakes. They're something that makes him feel comfortable—they're familiar. His whole life has been turned upside down in a matter of a month. He's moved to a different house, has a different room, a different nanny. You can't expect him to just move forward the way you are. He's little, and he doesn't understand. He needs time and patience to figure out what his world looks like now."

His face fell, and his shoulders sagged slightly.

"I'm fucking everything up."

"No, you're not," I said, stepping closer and resting a hand on his shoulder. I meant it to be comforting, but the way he looked at it with the heat in his eyes said that maybe it was sending a different message—one that both of us still wanted to act on.

I pulled away as if I'd been burned.

"I'm just saying that you need to cut him some slack and try to be a little more understanding. He's not trying to be difficult; he just wants things to be recognizable. He needs that right now."

"I thought I was doing a good thing," he laughed lightly. "He got up early, so I figured I would make breakfast before I needed to start my day. Guess the joke was on me."

I smiled and felt the heat in my cheeks as his eyes followed the curl of my lips.

"Don't worry about it. I'll make him the sprinkle pancakes and get the day going for him with a fun Christmas activity."

"Alright, thank you. There's plenty of boring pancakes if you want to help yourself."

"Thank you," I said as I reached into the cabinet on the other side of the stove to get the sprinkles out. "You can eat me anytime you'd like."

Once the words were out of my mouth, I felt the world around me spin when I realized what I had just said.

"I mean, feed me. You can *feed* me anytime you'd like," I corrected, avoiding looking at him as I set the container on the counter. My cheeks were flaming hot.

He gently brushed against me as he reached around to grab his cup of coffee. His hand rested lightly on my hip as he leaned in close to whisper so Alex couldn't hear him.

"I think I'd rather take you up on the first one."

My heart hammered against my chest as I tried to regain my composure before Alex returned.

Ten

Elliott

I pictured Sunny's lips wrapped around my cock as I fisted it in the bathroom, disappointed in myself for jerking off at 8:30 in the morning. That was what she did to me. It wasn't the first time I'd had to relieve myself since she started working for me, and at this rate, it wasn't going to be the last.

I pumped harder, holding myself up with one hand against the wall while the other stroked my thick shaft before I came into a handful of tissue.

My breathing was rapid and erratic as I tried to get the blood to flow through the rest of my body and not just my cock.

I opened the door, planning to head straight to my office when I ran into Sunny in the hallway. I'd purposely used the bathroom furthest away from them just to avoid having this happen.

It was hard to tell whether or not she knew what I had been doing, but the rosy, pink color in her cheeks suggested she might have been on to me.

"You have a package. I mean, I, um, signed for a package," she stammered, handing the box out to me.

I furrowed my brow for a second as I took it, then noticed the black tape with hot pink lettering that read Dark Vibes.

Our hands brushed against each other in the exchange, and I could swear I felt a vibration between us. Then I realized that it wasn't in my head and that the box was actually vibrating.

"Thank you." I rubbed my lips together, wondering how I was going to explain it. "It's from my work."

She nodded, but the blush just turned deeper.

"We're testing out a new product."

I watched as the color changed from pink to red as she tucked a strand of blonde hair behind her ear. She was freaking adorable when she blushed.

I hadn't talked to her about the line of work that I did, so this was setting up to be an awkward conversation. I could've avoided it and just headed to my office, but part of me wanted to see how she would react.

Pulling the pocket knife out of my pocket, I cut through the tape and opened the box. Her eyes watched with curiosity as I pulled the sleek pink vibrator out of the box and pressed the button to turn it off.

"It'll be part of our new product lineup for Mother's Day," I explained as if I weren't holding up a sex toy. "It's supposed to be extremely quiet, I guess I'll have to report back that it wasn't that quiet when I received it."

Her eyes looked up and locked on mine.

"We're looking for a few people to test it out for us. You can have this one if you're interested."

She swallowed hard, the movement in her throat pulling my eyes down and tempting me to look further at the way her nipples were pebbling beneath her shirt.

I wanted to lift her skirt, pull down her leggings, and try the vibrator out on her right now, but I couldn't. For one, Alex was awake and would only be distracted by the cartoon he was watching for a little bit. But two, she was still off limits, and I needed to remember that. I was flirting with danger but couldn't seem to stop myself.

"What do I have to do?" she asked quietly, her voice thick.

I licked my lips, biting back the words I really wanted to say.

"Use it and let me know what you like about it, what you don't like. All of our products are designed with women's satisfaction in mind, so I need to know if it's hitting the mark."

She reached up to take it from me, her fingers trembling slightly. I wrapped my hand around hers as she held it.

"I want you so fucking bad," I admitted, whispering quietly in her ear as my forehead rested against hers.

She was the one thing I wanted for Christmas, but the one gift I couldn't have.

"Think about me when you use it."

I didn't ask; I commanded and felt a rush when she simply nodded.

Slowly, I pulled away and dropped my hands to my side as I took the empty box and my raging erection back to my office and shut the door. *Why the fuck had I just admitted out loud that I wanted her?* I was losing it, and bad.

By lunchtime, I'd joined Sunny and Alex for a quick bite and then returned to my office. It wasn't that I didn't want to spend time with them, but that I didn't trust myself to be around Sunny. The kiss we shared last week was a constant reminder burning in the back of my head of what I wanted that I couldn't have.

Alex had taken to Sunny in no time, and they were practically inseparable now. He was constantly disappointed when she couldn't stay for dinner and didn't understand why she wasn't coming over and spending time with us on the weekend. While I loved that he felt so comfortable around her, I needed to make sure that I tried to keep what was left of the line clear so I didn't cross it again. I couldn't risk losing her because of stupidity on my part.

I was working through some emails in my office when I heard my phone ding with a new text message. I picked it up and found one from Sunny, asking if she could take Alex to Sugarplum Sweets. They were having a sugar cookie decorating class this afternoon, and she thought he might enjoy going and meeting some of the local kids around his age. Today's class was purposely designed for those under 5 years old who weren't in school.

I quickly responded, asking if she needed me to go with them. It wasn't that I didn't trust her to take him on her own, but part of me just didn't want to be excluded. I had a ton of work I needed to get done, but being around Sunny made it feel unimportant.

She responded with a simple smiley face after confirming

that she was fine to take him on her own but extended an invite if I wanted to take a break and join them.

Before I could think it through, I was marking myself out of the office and turning off my computer.

When I walked into the kitchen, she was helping Alex put on his jacket.

"Do you think the snow is going to keep falling?" he asked, looking up at her like she was an angel. Which, she was.

She leaned her head to the side a little bit and looked out the window.

"It sure looks like it."

"Maybe we'll have a white Christmas!" he said excitedly.

"I don't know, Buddy. Christmas is still three weeks away. That snow will probably melt by then," I answered, shoving my hands into my coat and smiling at my son as his face lit up when he saw me.

"Are you coming with us to decorate cookies?" he asked, his eyes wide with hope.

"I sure am!"

"We better get going, or we're going to be late," Sunny said, the warmth of her voice melting my stress away.

"Alright, let's go. I'll drive."

We all headed into the garage and piled into the SUV. I knew that Sunny was parked on the other side of the driveway and had thought about offering for her to park in the garage since it could easily fit three cars, and I only had one. But part of that felt weird, like it was something that a boyfriend would do, not her boss.

As I pulled out, I noticed the snow piled high on her car and knew that titles didn't matter anymore. There was no way in hell that I was going to have her outside, scraping ice and snow off of her car when it was already below freezing. I would take care of it for her tonight before she left, and then starting tomorrow, she would park in the garage and be comfortable coming and going from my house.

The car ride over was quick, but the sound of Sunny and Alex laughing about something that happened on one of his shows filled the silence. I grinned stupidly as I listened, wishing that I didn't have to miss these little moments with him that he was getting to enjoy with Sunny. It was weird, but I had never felt this jealous when he spent time with Magda. Then again, they didn't have the same kind of bond that he and Sunny had. It was different, but I couldn't put my finger on why.

I found a parking spot up front and turned the engine off. Sunny turned and smiled at me as she undid her seatbelt.

"Are you ready to go get messy?" she asked, the twinkle in her green eyes reminding me of lights dancing on a lit-up Christmas tree.

I narrowed my eyes at her and groaned. One week in, and she already knew how much I hated messes. Why had I thought this would be a good idea?

Eleven
Sunny

I tried to stifle my laughter as I sat next to Alex, who was already covered in glitter before we even got started. The look on Elliott's face as he worked his jaw back and forth while his hands twitched nervously as he debated whether to get them dirty was my undoing.

Andi continued with her instructions, which were more for the parents and not the toddlers who were already trying to eat their cookies before they decorated them. Thankfully, she knew a thing about toddlers and had set out a handful of broken ones that they could snack on before she handed out the reindeer and Santa ones we would be working with.

That's what I loved about Andi—that she loved kids as much as I did, which was probably why we'd been friends for so long. Sometimes I wondered if she did these classes because it was good for business or if she did them for me to have somewhere fun to take the kids I was watching. Either way, I liked being able to come here and have fun.

"You don't have to do this, you know," I whispered quietly when she was done.

Elliott looked over at me, a pained expression on his face as Alex giggled and tossed a handful of edible glitter in the air.

"Sugar Face Bar is right across the street. I can pick you up when we're done," I offered with a cheeky grin.

"I'm fine," he said on a heavy exhale.

"Yeah?" I arched an eyebrow in challenge. "Is that why your hands are still twitching under the table, afraid to come out and get dirty?"

I chewed my lip, wondering what his deal was with being messy. He was a control freak—there was no doubt about that. I even caught a small glimpse of it this morning when he offered me the vibrator and told me to think about him when I used it. Was I going to use it? Who knew? Would I think about him if I did? Ab-so-fucking-lutely.

"I was just trying to figure out how to get started." He pushed up the sleeves of his sweater, rolled his head back and forth on his neck, and looked like he was about to attempt a tedious surgery.

"Relax," I laughed. "Just start with the frosting. Pick a color and paint it on."

"Paint it on," he repeated without looking at me.

"Like this, Dad." Alex lifted his Santa cookie in the air to show him.

"See, even Alex can do it," I teased, hoping to lighten his mood.

Andi made her way back to our table and checked in, giving me a quick look that basically asked me what the deal was with Elliott as she frowned at the concerned look on his face while he picked out his frosting. I shrugged my shoulders and grinned.

She smiled back, but I could tell that she was dying to know more. Probably like why I was there with a parent and if there was something going on between us. I wished I could say there was, but Elliott had made it clear that there wasn't, even though him flirting with me sent completely different signals.

After she left, I returned my focus to Alex and helped him pick another color to add to his cookie. There was a plate of googly eyes and other decorations that we could add once we were ready.

I glanced over at Elliott, watching him out of the corner of my eye as he struggled with how to start frosting his cookie. Without thinking, I got up and stood behind him, reaching forward to help guide him. My breasts pressed into his muscular back, causing him to stiffen for a brief second before he took a long, heavy breath.

"Here, let me help you," I offered, wrapping my hands over his as he held the pastry bag filled with frosting. "Just press gently and squeeze down like this."

My breath hitched in my throat when I realized it looked like we were giving the damn bag a hand job. His fingers tightened around it, sliding slowly as the white frosting shot out onto the cookie, reminding me of what it might look like to see him cum.

I felt my face flush and knew that while my original intention was to be helpful, I was venturing into dangerous territory.

"There, that looks great." I pulled my hand away and stepped back, looking at the blob of white frosting sitting in the center of Santa's face.

"It looks like Santa got a *facial*," he muttered under his breath, making sure not to draw Alex's attention to us.

"I know," I whispered, covering my mouth before I burst into laughter. I couldn't help it; I laughed when I was nervous, and the blob that was now running down to where Santa's chin was didn't make it any better.

"What do I do now?" His voice was strained, but he did his best to keep it sounding cheery while Alex dusted some glitter onto his cookie.

"I don't know," I giggled. "Rub it in? Smear it around?"

He looked over his shoulder up at me.

"Is that what you would do?"

Our eyes locked, and I could tell he was no longer talking about the cookie.

"I wouldn't have let it happen in the first place," I said softly. "I'm not a messy girl."

Blue eyes darkened as if there was a storm now raging inside.

Before we could say anything more, Andi was headed our way and offered to help Elliott with his *situation*. What else could you call it at that point?

I took my seat next to Alex and tried to clear my head as I attempted to decorate an innocent little reindeer. This was supposed to be a fun activity for kids, not some erotic cookie-decorating class for horny adults. Though, that might be something to suggest to Andi when no one else was around.

After we finished decorating our cookies, Andi boxed them up and sent us on our way. I needed to stop by the store and grab a few things before the storm got worse, but I didn't want to ask Elliott to take me because I knew he was already missing work to be with Alex. But then again, it would be dark by the time I got off, and the roads would be worse to drive on.

I squirmed in my seat, anxiously chewing my nail while I debated what to do. As if tuned into my every movement, Elliott glanced at me and frowned before returning his focus to the icy, snow-packed road.

"What's wrong?" he asked as Alex sang along to a Christmas song from the back seat at the top of his lungs.

"Nothing," I lied, scrunching my shoulders and trying to hold in the gasp that escaped my throat as I felt the tires slip on a piece of ice. There was no way that I was going to feel comfortable enough going out in the storm tonight.

"You're a terrible liar," he commented, gripping the steering wheel tighter.

I let my shoulders sag and exhaled heavily.

"I need to go to the store tonight for some groceries, and I worry that the storm is going to get worse before I can make it."

His features pinched, making him look surprisingly sexy with the scowl on his face.

"Why didn't you ask me to take you? We're already out. It's easy to stop by the store, Sunny."

"Because I didn't want to inconvenience you. I know

you're already missing work to spend time with Alex today. I didn't want to put you further behind."

"I'm a grown man, Sunny. I can decide how I spend my time and am fully aware of my work responsibilities. If I say that it's okay, then it's okay."

I tugged at the sleeves of my sweater, feeling a slight chill spread through me. Again, as if aware of every single thing about me, Elliott reached over and turned the heat up on the seat warmer.

"Where did you need to go?"

"Whatever is easiest. I just need a few things."

"Does Sugarplum Market work?"

"Sure."

A few minutes later, we were parked and rushing inside with the last shopping cart. It was busy and packed for the middle of the day, which meant that everyone knew this storm was going to be a doozy, and they were stocking up.

I debated how much I should get and hated that I would still have to brave the icy roads to get to and from Elliott's house for the next few days since I lived on the other side of town. Elliott and Alex went on their way to grab a few groceries once Elliott realized that everyone else was stocking up too.

I made my way through the aisles, grabbing what I considered essentials: Diet Coke, BBQ chips, crackers, some cheese and sausage, lotion, fruit roll-ups, and some double-stuffed Oreos. Then I glanced out the window, noticing the heavy snow that was blanketing the parking lot, and grabbed a few bottles of wine.

Once I had my cart full, I made my way through the store and found Elliott and Alex with a cart they managed to snag and fill up with food while I was gone. I bit back the laughter when I realized the difference between him and me and what we considered to be the essentials.

Elliott's cart was filled with packs of meat, frozen vegetables, peanut butter, jelly, a couple of loaves of bread, snacks for Alex, bottles of water, Gatorade, and cereal—pretty much things that any responsible adult should be purchasing. There were even packs of facial tissue and toilet paper—two things that I needed but had forgotten about when I got distracted by the Oreos.

"Where do you live? We can drop this stuff off for you on the way back," Elliott offered, looking at the items in my cart but not commenting on any of them.

"It's okay," I rushed out. "I'm on the other side of town. I can take everything when I leave for the day. Thank you, though."

The lines between his eyebrows deepened, and he shook his head.

"What now?" I asked, planting my hand on my hip and meeting his eyes.

He worked his jaw back and forth, contemplating what he was going to say before he finally said it.

"I don't like the thought of you driving back and forth across town in this weather. It's not safe."

"What other options do I have?" I snorted. "The storm

isn't going to just stop because I have a job and need the money."

He glanced down at Alex and then back up at me.

"You'll stay with us."

He turned on his heel, ready to leave as if that was the final word.

"Excuse me?" I grabbed his arm and stopped him.

"You will stay with Alex and me until the storm passes and it's safe to leave."

My jaw dropped open, nearly hitting the floor.

"I can't do that," I said, slowly blinking in disbelief.

"Why not? You just said that you couldn't afford not to work. You work for me. I have a house with a guest room that isn't being used. What's the problem?"

I shook my head as I tried to figure out what it was— besides the fact that I couldn't imagine being cooped up in his house and *not* jumping his bones. Not that I could say that to him, though.

"I… umm…"

"Exactly." He reached his finger out and lifted my chin, closing my mouth. "Let's go before the storm gets worse. I imagine we'll need to grab a few things for you to wear while you're with us unless you happen to have a stash of clothes hiding in your car."

I frowned.

"I have a gym bag with some sweats and yoga pants."

I couldn't remember the last time I'd actually gone to the gym, but the bag was there, nonetheless.

His eyes quickly traveled down my body when I said *yoga pants,* and then a faint blush graced his cheeks.

"We'll pick up a few things, just to be safe." He cleared his throat and then headed to the women's clothing, straight to the baggy sweats.

I sighed heavily and then pushed my cart, following after him like the lost little desperate puppy I was.

Twelve
Elliott

"I'm sorry," I apologized, trying to shuffle the boxes around in the guest room to find the bed that hadn't been put together yet either. I'd completely forgotten that I hadn't gotten around to setting up the guest room since we moved in when I offered it to Sunny. Or maybe I was just leading with my dick again, and that's why I offered her to stay in a room I didn't technically have. It was like it had a mind of its own and was determined to keep her close by.

It was already late, and Alex was in bed, so I was trying to keep it down so I didn't wake him. The house was plenty big, but the five bedrooms were all next to each other at one end, and the walls were thinner than I would have liked.

"It's fine, don't worry," she assured me, tugging at the sleeves of her sweater again. It seemed to be a nervous habit that she was doing a lot around me lately. "I can go home; it's really not a big deal."

I stopped what I was doing and looked at her with my hands planted firmly on my hips.

"Like hell you will."

She rolled her eyes and leaned against the doorframe.

"I don't see what the big deal is. It's just snow. We get it all the time, I'll be fine."

"Yeah, and the six o'clock news reported that this is the worst storm Sugarplum Falls has seen in over twenty years. There's a freaking blizzard raging outside, Sunny," I said as I pointed to the window. "You're not leaving this house and driving in it."

"You can't really stop me." She scrunched her lips together in a way that had me wanting to bend her over my knee so I could paddle her ass.

"Try me."

Within seconds, I was across the room, invading her space as I lifted her chin and pinched it between my fingers.

"You may think that you can handle the storm, but I can guarantee you that you can't handle me when I don't get my way."

A small gasp escaped her throat as her tongue slowly slid out to lick her lips.

I wanted to reach down and kiss her, to press my aching cock into her tight, wet folds. I wanted to do things that I wasn't allowed to do, and that was even more frustrating than her wanting to leave.

"You'll sleep in my bed," I blurted out as I let go of her chin and stepped back to draw in a breath of fresh air.

Her eyes widened as her head pulled back.

"Not with me." I felt the sting of heat pinch my cheeks. "I'll sleep on the couch, and you'll take my bed."

I turned and walked out of the room before she could object.

I had no idea what had come over me. It wasn't like me to act this way or to be so reckless. I'd built myself an empire based on sound decisions and well-thought-out plans. Now, all of a sudden, I couldn't think straight and was offering my bed to my way too young nanny, who I desperately wanted to fuck. People were right—Sugarplum Falls did something to you.

By the time I got the stuff I needed from my room, Sunny was already asleep on the couch. I grunted in frustration and debated whether I should carry her to my bed or be the jerk who woke her up when she looked like she was sleeping so peacefully.

I grabbed the blanket from the back of the couch and covered her, hating that she was sleeping there instead of someplace more comfortable—like my bed. It didn't feel right to go back to my room when I had already offered it to her, but then again, I didn't want to be a creeper and sleep on the other couch. I was standing there, with a ridiculously stupid battle playing in my head, when she spoke softly.

"Go to bed, Elliott. I'm fine on the couch."

Her eyes were still closed, and I could tell she was already drifting back to sleep when she sunk deeper into the pillow and let out a soft moan as she stretched to get comfortable.

I puffed my cheeks with the hot air that needed to come out, then went to my room. It was going to be a long, sleepless night.

The next morning, I woke up with painful morning wood and groaned, knowing that it would be hard to deal with it with Sunny in the house. Not that I hadn't jacked off already while she was here, but I wasn't proud of it. It was like I was reduced to a horny teenager who had no control of his body or the desires coursing through it. I got up, checked to make sure that Alex was still asleep, and jumped in the shower.

It was Wednesday, which meant that we had our weekly team meeting, and I wasn't in the mood for it. I hadn't slept well and felt cranky and irritated. After I got ready, I crept into the kitchen to start a pot of coffee while trying not to wake Sunny up.

When I walked in, I found her leaning against the counter, lifting the new coffee mug I bought her to her lips as she took a sip.

"There's a fresh pot ready," she offered, lifting her cup toward it. "I also have a quiche baking in the oven and can bring you some once it's ready. What time is your meeting?"

I glanced at the clock on the stove as I poured myself a cup of coffee.

"In twenty minutes."

"Okay, just text me when you're ready, and I'll bring you some food. I don't want to interrupt."

"Thank you."

I hated that she was cooking for me, but once I smelled the heavenly aroma floating in the air around us, I felt that anger dissipate.

"You're up early," I commented before taking a sip.

"I'm used to getting up before most people. A lot of the families I've nannied for have had early days, so it's just part of my routine now."

"Did you sleep okay?"

She nodded and took another drink.

"I think your couch might be more comfortable than my bed," she joked.

I took another drink, washing down the urge to offer her to sleep on it permanently.

"I better get going," I said, nodding to my office. "It'd be bad if the boss was late to his own meeting."

She smiled as I turned and walked away, hating that I was going to work and not spending time with her instead. I knew that she was having quite the impact on Alex, but I hadn't realized just how big of one she was having on me.

I sat down at my desk and got situated. It was less than three weeks until Christmas, and we were still trying to crank out the new vibrators after the whole wiring debacle we had last week. My team had worked overtime to get us back on track, but we were still a few days behind where we should have been.

We had preorders lined up, and our warehouse was ready to get started on shipping, but I needed updates that everything had been taken care of and that the product we were about to send out was our best yet. The last thing I wanted or needed was to rush this, send something less than stellar out, and tank our reputation. I'd worked too hard for too long to get myself in the position I was in and risk losing it over something stupid and avoidable.

I turned the volume up on my speakers and started the Zoom meeting, sipping my coffee while I waited for the rest of the team to join. It was all upper management, including those at the manufacturer we worked with.

A few minutes later, everyone was online, and we were ready to begin. Malcolm, the executive director, took the lead and gave me updates on where things were. I listened as Giana jumped in and provided an update on the wiring issue and the quality control checks that were currently being completed. It was a massive job that was requiring her team to work overtime, but she assured me that they were at least 75% done and would be wrapped up by the end of the day.

I made a note to give her a large holiday bonus this year, as well as her staff. They were busting their assess to get this done and deserved to be rewarded for their hard work. This was on top of the regular bonuses that would be going out to all of my employees next week. I did well, but I never forgot that my success was due to the dedication of my team. I had a very low turnover rate and made sure to compensate my employees above what they would find elsewhere. I wanted the best of the best, and I was willing to pay for it.

Half an hour later, we finished the meeting, and I felt a weight lifted from my shoulders, knowing that the vibrators would get out in time. We had an increase in pre orders overnight, which was due to an online influencer promoting the one she got early on as a tester. I jotted down another note to send her a thank-you gift as well. The sales that came in with the promo code we gave her to use had generated at least five thousand additional orders, which meant that this year we would exceed sales from any previous year.

I was busy sending an email when I heard my phone ding

with a notification. I picked it up and found a text message from Sunny, reminding me to let her know when I was ready for breakfast. My fingers moved quickly over the screen, letting her know I was done but would be out in a few minutes to join her and Alex for breakfast. Sure, I still had a ton of work to do and needed to catch up from my time off yesterday, but I could stop for a quick meal.

When I got to the kitchen, Sunny was sitting at the table with Alex, her head back as she laughed at something he said. His grin spread from ear to ear, lighting up his little face. My heart warmed at the sight, and I tried to ignore the thoughts that were spreading through my mind about how this looked like the perfect family.

"Hey," she said cheerfully when she saw me. "Let me grab your food."

She got up and went to the oven, bending over as the tight yoga pants stretched across her ass, and pulled out the plate she was keeping warm for me.

"Do you want some juice?" She set the food in front of me, her breasts brushing against my back in the process. I could tell that it impacted her as much as it did me when I felt the hard pebble of her nipples through the thin t-shirt she was wearing.

We had gone back and forth yesterday at the store, with me trying to get her to buy loose *old lady* sweats, but she insisted that she was more comfortable in yoga pants, leggings, and t-shirts. Since I couldn't force her to wear something she didn't want to, I decided to put my foot down on buying her stuff for her. It was a brief battle but won easily when Alex batted his eyes at her and asked her to let his daddy help her. He had no idea what was going on, but I appreciated him being able to melt her hard exterior for a few minutes so I could get my way. I knew that she was already worried about money, and the last thing I wanted was for her to feel the strain of spending what she did have on new clothes because I was forcing her to stay with me to keep her safe.

I cleared my throat and went to get up when her hand on my shoulder stopped me.

"I'll get it for you, just let me know what you want."

You. Naked. On my bed. My cock buried deep inside of you. You calling my name. Scratching your nails down my back. Panting as I plunge harder, fucking you with everything I've got.

"Apple juice would be great, thanks."

I couldn't tell if my voice was actually as thick and gruff as it sounded or if the words were just easily getting caught in my throat.

She shuffled around the kitchen, humming a song under her breath, then set a glass of juice in front of me and sat down as if she hadn't just shifted my world on its axis.

Couldn't she feel the energy between us? Wasn't this impacting her the same way it was me? How could she just sit there as if there wasn't this electrifying energy coursing between us?

I decided to keep my mouth occupied and started eating before I could say something stupid. Alex was telling Sunny another story about a cotton ball snowman that he saw on TV and asked if she could help him make one. She nodded enthusiastically and promised they would do some crafts this morning after he finished his breakfast.

I hadn't noticed until now that he was eating his own mini quiche and wondered how in the world Sunny had pulled that off. I couldn't get Alex to eat half of the stuff she did.

"What are you eating, Buddy?" I asked, smiling as I nodded to his plate.

"Sunny made me a baby keechy."

I raised my eyebrows and started laughing as Sunny joined in.

"It's a quiche," she said gently. "But that's a big word, and you did a great job saying it!"

"Do you like it?" I asked as he shoved another bite in his mouth.

He nodded and grinned like a goofball.

"It's ham and cheese," Sunny offered. "And a little bit of spinach to help build his superpowers because *all heroes* need their super strength."

Alex pulled his brows together and lifted his arm, attempting to show me his tiny muscles.

"There's spinach in yours, too," she offered. "It'll give you some energy this morning since you had such a restless night."

I arched an eyebrow, wondering how in the hell she knew that I was restless.

"The walls are thin, and I was up a few times to use the

restroom." She shrugged as if it were no big deal that she was basically admitting that she *heard* how restless I was given that the bathroom she used shared a wall with my bedroom, and my bed just so happened to be close to it.

A faint blush crept up my cheeks as I forked another bite of quiche into my mouth. It was delicious, but I couldn't concentrate on any of that while I sat there, mortified that she heard me jacking off last night. *Had she heard her name on my lips? Did you get disgusted and walk away? Did she get curious and use that vibrator I gave her?*

Suddenly, I felt the blood rushing to my groin. I shoved the last few bites into my mouth, took a long drink of juice, and then got up and set my dirty dishes in the sink.

"I've gotta get back to work," I announced awkwardly, shuffling my hand through Alex's hair as he tried to squirm away.

"Daaadddd," he groaned, ducking away from my reach.

"I'll see you in a few hours for lunch. Be good for Sunny."

I didn't listen as they spoke, I just headed straight to my office and forced myself to get my head in the game and away from thoughts of Sunny.

Thirteen
Sunny

The first few days of staying with Elliott were more awkward than I would have imagined. It was weird because even though he insisted that I stay with them, he seemed overly stressed out about it. He was constantly brash, and his stress levels seemed to escalate over the first forty-eight hours I was there.

I had offered to go home several times and then stopped when I noticed how it only seemed to agitate him more. The storm ended up being worse than the local weatherman had predicted, and I was actually thankful that I didn't have to travel back and forth across town in it. Even though Sugarplum Falls was used to the snow, they hadn't had it dump this much in such a short amount of time and weren't equipped to deal with it.

Alex and I were having a great time, and I enjoyed being there when he woke up in the morning. It was easier than rushing over in the morning and feeling antsy if I was running late. By already being there, I was able to get the day going without feeling any stress or pressure to get caught up or to get the day started. I found myself wondering what it would be like if that were my life and hated the disappointed feeling that washed over me when I realized that it would never happen. Although Elliott had been sending a lot mixed signals since I started working for him, us not crossing the line was the one thing that had been made clear.

This morning it felt different to wake up and know that it was technically my last day of work since it was Friday and Elliott hadn't needed me to watch Alex on the weekends yet. The weather was still bad, and I knew that he wasn't going to let me leave to go home after I was officially off of the clock tonight, but I wasn't sure what that meant for the weekend. I would be here with them, invading their space, but it would be as a guest and not as a paid employee. My nerves started to get the worst of me when I wondered whether he would still want me to stay with them if I weren't being paid to care for his son.

I was in the kitchen, cleaning up from breakfast while Alex watched his favorite cartoon when Elliott came in and refilled his coffee.

We worked around each other, silently moving without touching, but I could almost hear the sizzling and crackling of the energy between us whenever we got close to each other. It was such a constant thing that I found myself wanting to be next to him, just to get that jolt of electricity from him.

It was as exciting as it was nerve-wracking, and I was starting to get frustrated with all the built-up tension I had lingering inside. If I were at home, in the comfort of my own room, I would have grabbed a bottle of wine and used the vibrator Elliott gave me at the beginning of the week. I'd thought about it a time or two, but it wasn't like I was going to just get myself off on his couch or tie up the bathroom and risk him hearing me like I heard him the first night I stayed over—which was freaking hot and only further frustrated me.

Once he was finished and had what he needed, I let out a sigh of relief and leaned against the sink, resting my head on the cabinet.

"Everything okay?" a low voice startled me, forcing me to spin around.

My hand flung to my chest as my eyes widened in surprise to see him standing there, casually watching me with his hands shoved in the pockets of his dark faded jeans.

"Yeah," I said quickly, trying to regain my composure. "I thought you went back to your office."

"I did. But then I forgot my phone, so I came back."

I glanced behind him to see it sitting on the counter.

"So," he said slowly, folding his arms over his broad, tight chest. "What's wrong?"

"Nothing," I lied, looking away from him as I worried my lower lip between my teeth.

"Sunny."

He gave me a pointed look, my name a warning on his lips.

Blood rushed through my head, making me feel intoxicated. Or maybe that was just the effect Elliott had on me.

One eyebrow lifted, but he didn't make any other movement, frozen in place as he waited for me to cave and give in to what he wanted.

I shrugged and tried to stop fidgeting.

"The news said that the storm is supposed to get worse today."

"And?"

"And it's Friday." I raised my eyebrows as if that should be enough to explain the problem.

"What does that have to do with anything?"

I sighed heavily and picked up the towel I had been using to dry the dishes, twisting it between my hands.

"Because I'm officially off the clock at five."

"You're not leaving and driving in this. If you *have* to go, then Alex and I will take you home. But you're not attempting to go home by yourself with the roads as dangerous as they are."

"I'm not going to have you take Alex out in this," I shrieked, the thought of him putting him in harm's way just to take me home made me nauseous. "That would be incredibly dangerous and stupid."

"I'm glad we finally agree on something."

"But I can't just keep staying here," I insisted. "I get that it worked well during the week because you needed someone to take care of Alex, but you're off this weekend, so you don't need me here."

"That doesn't mean that we don't want you here."

My heart fluttered in my chest as I instantly replayed his words in my head.

"I don't know…"

He continued to study me, then turned his head slightly toward Alex while keeping his eyes locked on mine.

"Hey, Buddy," he called out.

"Yeah?"

"Do you want to make pizza tonight and play a game?"

"Yes!"

"Do you want Sunny to stay and join us?"

"Yes!"

"Do you think she should stay the night again since the snow is really bad and it's not safe for her to drive in it?"

"Yes!"

"Should we wake up tomorrow morning and build a snowman? Then come inside and warm up by the fire with some hot chocolate?"

"Yes! Yes! Yes!"

I tried to keep from grinning about how excited Alex was, but I failed miserably.

"There you go, problem solved." He lowered his voice so only I could hear him, tossed a wink over his shoulder, and headed back to his office. "By the way, smiling looks good on you."

My stomach twisted in nervous knots, my heart battling my mind over trying not to obsess over what he'd just said.

The rest of the day felt like a blur after that. Alex and I did some more arts and crafts, and then I made sure to clean up the mess before Elliott saw it. I knew how anal he was about keeping things clean and organized, though I couldn't stop imagining what it would look like if he just gave in and relinquished the control he was constantly holding in a vice grip.

By four o'clock, Elliott was done with work and came padding down the hallway, barefoot, wearing jeans and a graphic t-shirt that pulled tightly across his chest. He had changed from the sweater he had on earlier, and I couldn't help but notice how his body looked in this outfit.

We all shuffled about in the kitchen, assembling our individual pizzas while Christmas carols played in the background. I laughed and giggled as Alex convinced Elliott to make a snowman out of his and then piled a ginormous amount of mozzarella cheese on the dough to make it into a beard.

They seemed to be enjoying themselves as they added toppings, giving the snowman pepperoni eyes and a mouth made out of sliced bell pepper. It was adorable, and I truly loved seeing them bond together.

My pizza started out simple until Elliott looked over and noticed it was just basic and plain. He frowned, shook his head, and told Alex that they were going to have to show me how to make a Christmas pizza.

The next thing I knew, both of them were on either side of me, adding a handful of shredded cheese and bell pepper—two of my favorite toppings—until there was a definite snowflake-looking shape on mine. I smiled proudly and tried to ignore how Elliott's body felt pressed against mine as he stood behind me and guided my hands as we worked.

My body was on high alert, feeling every shift in energy as he moved around me. I also felt the impact it was having on him when he let his erection graze my ass a few times through the thin fabric of my leggings.

Alex went to wash up while Elliott and I cleaned the mess from the kitchen table and got it ready for dinner.

"Do you want some eggnog?" he offered, gently placing a hand on my lower back as he leaned in to toss a napkin in the trash.

I pulled my shoulders back, my body instantly stiffening beneath his touch as I craved more but didn't want to risk acting on it and having Alex come in and catch us.

"Umm…" I scrunched my face while I considered whether I should or not.

"You're officially off the clock now, Sunny," he teased. "You can enjoy some eggnog and relax. You're our guest, not my employee."

I licked my lips, my mouth suddenly feeling super dry.

"Are you going to have some?"

Something flickered in his eyes, but I couldn't tell what it was.

"I am."

"Okay," I nodded quickly as my heart raced again. How in the world did he have such an impact on me without doing anything?

I had forgotten that he'd bought the eggnog when we'd shopped earlier in the week and hadn't thought about it again until now. Suddenly, I was thankful for the liquid courage that I was going to need to relax around him.

I tried to calm my nerves as he opened the bottle and poured each of us a glass while I washed the veggies for the salad. It wasn't like this was the first time I'd stayed for dinner with him and Alex, but tonight felt different. It felt like a first date, and I couldn't stop myself from getting excited about it.

Fourteen
Elliott

Dinner with Sunny was fun and relaxing after she finished her eggnog and stopped looking like a terrified deer caught in the headlights. I wasn't sure what was making her so nervous, but I could tell that it had something to do with me. Given that I knew women's bodies pretty well, I was going to go out on a limb and guess that she was feeling as aroused around me as I was around her. The only problem was that we both knew that we couldn't act on it, even though it would feel fucking amazing if we did.

Never in my life had I been so sexually frustrated.

It was like I constantly had a raging boner and was looking for something to shove it into. Okay, not just *something*. Sunny. I wanted to shove it into the beautiful, young nanny I'd hired to care for my child. I wanted to fuck her tight little pussy and watch as her plump lips wrapped around my cock as she took me into the back of her throat. I wanted to have her ride my cock and use it to bring herself to orgasm. I wanted to taste her and devour every single inch of her body, licking up the wetness of her arousal.

But I couldn't have any of that, which was beyond frustrating.

The night went well, and we played a few games with Alex until it was time for him to go to bed. I could tell that he was tired, even if he fought it. I assured him that Sunny would be there in the morning and that we would build snowmen and then enjoy some hot chocolate by the fire when we were done. He was getting so used to having Sunny constantly at our house that I worried about how he would react when the storm passed and she didn't have to stay with us anymore.

It might've been a dick thing to think, but deep down, I was hoping Mother Nature had more in store for us, and we'd get hit with another couple of feet of snow just to keep her at my house longer. Even if it was torture having her there and not being able to touch her, I still wanted to have her there.

By the time I got Alex down, it was still early, and I wasn't sure what to do. Usually, I would watch TV in the living room or work in my office, but neither of those sounded feasible tonight. My mind was too scattered, consumed with thoughts of Sunny, to be able to focus on work. And given that she was still sleeping on the couch, it felt weird to invite myself back in there to watch TV.

I walked quietly into the kitchen and filled a glass of water while I tried to decide what to do. Sunny was curled up on the couch with a blanket covering her lap while she watched TV. I guzzled down the water and then refilled another glass.

"Do you want to come watch a movie?" she offered, smiling at me from across the room.

I cleared my voice and pulled my shoulders back. This shouldn't be a hard decision, so why did it feel like I couldn't answer her?

"Sure," I finally blurted out before setting my glass down and heading to the couch.

She lifted the blanket, waited for me to sit beside her, and then covered me with the extra fabric. It felt wrong to be under the blanket with Sunny, but it wasn't like we were doing anything. It was simply chilly in the house and snowing outside. It made sense that we would want to keep warm.

Keep telling yourself those lies, dumbass.

"What do you want to watch?" she asked, offering me the remote.

"Whatever you pick is fine," I replied stoically as I kept my attention on the TV and my body rigid next to hers.

She pulled her mouth to the side and thought about it as she flipped through channels.

"Do you want action or Christmas or comedy?"

"Anything is fine with me."

She sighed loudly—making sure I heard her—and then continued to scroll through the options until she decided on an action flick.

I tried my best to relax and enjoy the movie, but I couldn't stop focusing on the heat coming from her body. It didn't help that I'd changed after getting Alex down, and the gray sweatpants I had on did nothing to try to contain the hard-on that wanted to make a grand appearance.

Sunny was wearing some thin leggings that wrapped so tightly around her ass that I thought I was going to bust a nut at dinner. Helping her with her pizza was heaven and hell as I grazed against her ass and knew she could feel my erection when she softly gasped and arched her body into mine.

The movie was playing, but I had no idea what was happening. Sunny sat beside me, chewing her fingernail as she watched. It was an intense scene, but I couldn't tell you why. I just knew that the music suddenly changed from suspenseful to something that sounded a bit like porn. I forced myself to pay attention and found a couple clawing at each other's clothes as they ripped them off and flung them across the room.

The guy was attractive and built with a six-pack stomach that the girl was running her tongue down before he lifted her by her ass and pinned her to a wall. He pulled her shirt up and over her head, revealing a sexy lace bra that I could imagine being something that Sunny would wear.

Normally, I would find myself interested in what was happening on the screen, but I couldn't stop thinking about it being Sunny and me instead. Her eyes were still locked on the TV when I felt her hand move across my thigh and brush against my cock.

My body tightened as I held my breath, not willing to move or do anything. Her fingers ran along the outside before she gripped it and tugged slightly.

I involuntarily let out a small moan with the breath I was holding.

She turned slowly to look at me, lower lip pulled between her teeth as her green eyes sparkled with lust.

"Sunny." Everything was strained as I fought to control myself and not act on this.

"Hmmm?"

"You're gripping my—ahem."

Her grin spread tightly across her face as she pretended to be shocked by the news.

"Oops. I thought it was the remote."

I swallowed hard, my Adam's apple bobbing.

"Is that your way of saying you're trying to turn me on?"

It was a corny joke, and I regretted saying it the moment it left my mouth.

She giggled and rubbed me slowly, forcing all the blood out of my head and straight to my groin.

"Maybe. Is it working?"

Her voice was flirtier than I'd ever heard before, and it was doing more damage to any resolve I had left.

"You tell me."

I was still straining, trying to find the strength to stop this as she continued rubbing me.

"It's hard to tell with this blanket in the way. Maybe I can get a better look?"

Before I could respond, she had ducked beneath it and was bent over my lap with her head lined up above my cock. Her hand quickly freed me from my clothes as she pulled the sweats down around me. I closed my eyes and leaned my head back on the couch as she slowly licked the tip before taking me into her mouth.

It was wrong to let this happen but fuck if it didn't feel right. Her mouth was magical, taking me deep into the back of her throat, sucking hard as her hand wrapped tightly around the length that didn't fit.

It was warm, wet, and inviting, making it impossible to pull away and tell her to stop.

As if sensing the war raging inside my head, she pulled away for a quick second, popped out of the blanket, and told me to relax before she resumed her position, sucking my cock.

I kept the blanket off her head, so she didn't suffocate, but more so I could watch her. She looked just as great as I imagined she would giving head, but it wasn't enough. I wanted more. I wanted to taste her. To feel her pussy grip me as it spasmed around me as she came. But could any of that happen? We'd already crossed one line, and there was no going back. Not only that, I didn't have to worry about whether or not she wanted this as she eagerly sucked every last drop of cum out of me as I released into her mouth and shot my load down the back of her throat.

Once I was done, she sat up and gently wiped the sides of her mouth before turning back to the TV and pretending that nothing had just happened.

I waited a few seconds for the blood to spread through the rest of my body again before I got up and went to my office. When I came back, Sunny seemed surprised to see me.

I held out a thin black box and handed it to her.

"What's this?" she asked, taking it from me.

"You'll see."

Fifteen
Sunny

I opened the box and gasped when I saw a small vibrator-looking toy inside. It wasn't a straight, penis-type one like the ones I was used to. Instead, it looked like it was bent in half. I imagined it clamping down on my most sensitive parts.

"It's my turn," Elliott said quietly as he sat on the couch beside me and pushed the blanket off. "Lay down."

I stared at him in disbelief as he took the box from my hand and pulled the toy out.

"Lay down, Sunny."

Something about the way he commanded me to do it made it that much hotter, and I found myself lying back on the pillow behind me.

"This is the Dark Vibes G-Shocker. It's designed to stimulate your clit and g-spot at the same time."

My eyes widened, not sure how I felt about it.

"You helped with my pent-up frustration; now it's time to take care of yours."

He licked his lips as he set the toy down and leaned forward, hovering over me as he slid his fingers into the waistband of my leggings.

"Can I?"

I nodded. Words were completely useless at this point as all my brain power was focused on how his hands felt as they touched me.

A slight chill in the air nipped at my skin as soon as I was relieved of my pants. I had on black cotton boy short panties, and while I hadn't been planning for Elliott to see me in them, I didn't necessarily mind that they weren't overly sexy when I saw the way he was looking at me.

"These too," he said, hooking his fingers into them before pulling them down.

Once I was fully exposed before him, I tried to press my legs together, but he shook his head and pushed them apart.

"I've had blue balls for a week, Sunny. I'm not going to miss seeing this."

My heart raced wildly in my chest as his eyes traveled over my body while his fingers skimmed over my skin.

"There are so many things I want to do to this sexy little body of yours. But first, I want to watch you come."

I tried to mutter a word, but a moan came out instead. I was already wet and turned on, and he hadn't even touched me where I needed him to yet.

His fingers glided over my hip, tickling me with their soft touch. Then they dipped lower, brushing over my pussy but not stopping where I wanted them.

I arched my back and shifted to bring him closer, but he

pulled away and chuckled instead.

"So anxious for me to touch you, aren't you?"

I nodded, my breathing coming in labored pants.

"I shouldn't be doing this," he muttered, allowing his fingers to trail back over my pussy. His middle finger slid across my slit, teasing me before he finally pushed it inside.

I gasped and bucked off of the couch. My body was on fire, and I was ready for this. Hell, I was ready for more—much, much more.

"It feels too good to stop," he continued. "But fuck if I don't want more, Sunny."

"Ahhhh," I cried as he slid another finger inside me. I knew he wanted to use the toy, but honestly, all I needed at this point was for him to touch my clit, and I would be coming in seconds.

I was wound so tightly that I wanted nothing more than the release heading my way. I wasn't too proud to take what I wanted, even if it meant that I needed to climb onto his hand and rub myself against it until I got off. I would hump whatever I had to at this point just to get what was shaping up to be one of the best orgasms of my life.

"I know you want more too. We're going to make you feel really good here in just a few, I promise. Right now, I just want to feel your tight pussy as she grips me. You're so wet for me, Sunny. So fucking wet."

His words were about to send me over the edge, I was so close.

"Please, Elliott. Please. Please. Please," I begged

repeatedly, hoping he would have mercy and put me out of my misery.

"Be a good girl and put this inside of you," he instructed, pulling his fingers out and handing me the toy.

My brain was too foggy to focus. I stared at him dumbly, not having any idea what he wanted from me. Why couldn't he just use his damn fingers to get me off? I was almost there.

He grinned and seemed to notice my current state as he did the honor of putting the toy inside of me.

I leaned back and tried to relax as I got used to the feeling of it. One end was inside of me, pressing against the wall, while the other wrapped around and had a vibrating nub that pressed firmly against my clit.

"Are you ready?" he asked.

I nodded eagerly, though I really had no idea what to expect.

He pulled a remote control out of the box and leaned back as he watched me. Suddenly, I felt a jolt as the toy started vibrating inside of me.

I closed my eyes and gripped the blanket beneath me as I tried to get used to the sensation, even though my body was already on overload.

I was climbing my way back to the orgasm I was just on the cusp of having when I heard Alex's little voice.

"Daddy, I need a drink of water," he said sleepily as he rubbed his eyes.

Elliott was quicker than me and had me covered under the blanket before Alex got to us.

"Hey, Buddy. Let's get a quick drink and then go back to bed."

He got up and tucked the control into his pocket as I tried to shift on the couch to make it less obvious that something was happening. The toy was still firmly placed inside of me, pressing harder against my clit as I adjusted to a sitting position.

Elliott grabbed a glass and filled it with water before giving it to Alex. As he was drinking, he dropped the stuffed animal that he always slept with. When Elliott bent down to grab it, he must have put pressure on the remote because suddenly, the toy was on again and at full speed.

"Ahhhh!" I yelped from the couch, drawing both of their attention over to me.

I curled into the couch and tried to cover my face as I fought off the orgasm that wanted to come out. There was no way that it was happening right now.

"What's wrong with Sunny?" Alex asked as he gave the glass back to Elliott, who was staring at me in confusion as I writhed beneath the torture of the toy.

Suddenly, it must have clicked because he rushed out a quick, bullshit excuse.

"Oh, she has a stomachache. Must have been too much junk food tonight," he lied, leading his son out of the room and away from me.

But before they could get very far, Alex turned and looked at me.

I tried to keep my face expressionless while Elliott worked on turning off the toy.

"You probably need to poop," Alex said, rubbing his eyes again. "That's what I do when my tummy hurts. Just poop, and you'll feel better."

I nodded and gave him a thumbs-up while Elliott ushered him back to his room.

A few minutes later, Elliott was back and sat beside me on the couch.

"I'm so sorry about that," he apologized.

"I'm not sure what was worse—being interrupted by Alex or almost coming with him in the room. That toy is incredibly powerful."

"I know," he laughed. "Alex rarely ever gets up, so that was an unexpected surprise. He should be down for the rest of the night now. And yes, the toy packs a lot of power which is why it's my favorite."

I didn't want to jump down a rabbit hole I couldn't get out of, so I didn't bother to ask him how he knew. There were way too many questions that would come from that.

"Are you okay?" he asked softly.

"Yeah. I feel like my body doesn't know what to do. I keep getting so close to having one, and then it's gone."

"Edging can be fun when it's done intentionally and not like this," he laughed.

"Edging?"

I didn't want to sound stupid or naïve, but I seriously had no idea what he was talking about.

He closed his eyes and scrubbed a hand down his face as he spoke.

"Remind me how old you are again."

"I'm twenty-three. But I'm not a virgin or anything; you don't have to panic."

He opened his eyes and looked at me.

"No, but I'm quite a bit older and forget that you haven't been doing things as long as I have."

I felt better with his gentle tone and didn't feel like he was treating me like some inexperienced idiot.

"So, what is it?"

He pulled his head back for a moment before remembering what we were talking about.

"Edging is where you stop yourself from coming when you're right on the cusp. You do it repeatedly, and it builds the intensity of the orgasm."

I could still feel the toy inside of me, but I didn't feel like I was going to burst into flames if I didn't come right away like I had a few seconds before Alex walked in.

"Oh. I see. Well, I'm not sure that it worked because I don't even feel it building anymore."

I shrugged as if it were no big deal that I had missed out on at least two tonight.

"Not to worry, it'll be a damn good release once you get it."

"Oh no, I'm fine," I lied as I laughed nervously. "I don't need one. In fact, I was going to go to the bathroom to take it ouuu--- HOLY FUCK!"

I leaned back into the cushion and gripped the fabric of the blanket that was still covering me. Elliott watched me intently as he pressed the button again, making the vibration stronger.

"What were you saying?" he asked smugly, chewing his bottom lip.

"I, I," I panted, desperate for the orgasm that was working its way through me again. "Oh my God!"

I tried to be quiet, but it was damn near impossible when Elliott increased it again. I couldn't decide which way my body wanted to go and found myself turning so Elliott could see what he was doing to me.

"Come for me, Sunny."

As if I needed any further coaxing, I threw my head back and squeezed my legs together, riding out the strongest orgasm I'd ever had. I felt a gush rush out of me but couldn't bother to stop and care as I spasmed against the toy, feeling it drain every last bit out of me before Elliott turned it off.

I was still panting, trying to catch my breath, when I finally opened my eyes and looked at him.

"So, how was it?"

I reached beneath the blanket and pulled it out, noticing the mess I'd made. My cheeks flushed with embarrassment when I saw the wet spot beneath me.

"It was fucking amazing. I'm so sorry, I think I made a mess."

He took the toy and stood, extending his hand to help me up.

"Don't ever apologize about that. It's sexy watching you come undone, and I would've never pegged you for a squirter. Now that I know that it's going to be fucking impossible to keep my hands off of you."

He grabbed the blanket and the toy, taking them to the sink while I went to the bathroom to clean up. My legs felt wobbly, and my body was the most relaxed it had ever been.

102

BLAME IT ON THE EGGNOG

Sixteen
Elliott

Was I wrong for what happened between Sunny and me last night? Maybe. Did I regret it? Not one fucking bit.

We got up early this morning and enjoyed a cup of coffee together while we waited for Alex to get up. Neither of us talked about last night, but I could tell things between us had shifted. For one, Sunny was nowhere as nervous around me as she had been before, and I found myself a lot more relaxed than I had been in years.

Sure the blow job probably helped with that, but there was more to it. I hadn't dated since Sharon and I separated because there was never any time, given that I was a single dad and worked sixty hours a week. Magda was good and I was worried that we wouldn't find someone in Sugarplum Falls to replace her, but now that we had Sunny, I couldn't imagine anyone else.

Alex was the happiest that I had ever seen him, and I felt like things in our life were finally settling down and becoming easier. Thanks to Sunny, I found myself putting work to the side more often than not so I could spend time with Alex and enjoy these moments before he started school and they were gone. Magda never bothered to fix me anything to eat and kept her focus on Alex during the day, which in all fairness was what I expected of her and paid her to do.

On the other hand, Sunny seemed to adore Alex and genuinely enjoyed spending time with him. They had so many inside jokes, and she understood him better than I did sometimes. She was such a bubbly personality that she automatically brightened up things around the house. Not only that, it felt natural to have her there with us, almost like we were one big happy family. The time she'd spent staying over only solidified that thought more in my head, making it harder to accept that she would be gone as soon as the storm passed and the roads were clear.

We were sitting on the couch, watching TV, when Alex finally woke up and joined us.

"Good morning, Buddy," I said as I ruffled his hair.

"Daaaddd," he groaned, ducking away as he swatted at me.

I laughed and saw the smile plastered on Sunny's face.

"You want to go build snowmen this morning?" I asked, knowing that this would be the thing to get him excited this morning.

His blue eyes lit up, and his grin was so tight I worried it might hurt. He nodded his head and then jumped up and down excitedly.

"Alright, go use the bathroom, and then I'll help you get your snow gear on."

He took off running down the hall and shut the bathroom door behind him.

"I love his enthusiasm," Sunny said as she followed me into the kitchen and set her coffee mug in the sink next to mine. She turned to move, but I snaked my arm around her waist and pinned her to the counter instead.

"He's a kid who knows what he wants."

She raised an eyebrow and ran her hands up my arms until they locked around my neck.

It felt good to hold her, and I found myself not wanting to stop.

"Just like his dad."

"Mmmhmm," I murmured as I leaned in to kiss the side of her neck. My dick was already hard, growing faster than the Grinch's heart when he found out the true meaning of Christmas.

"I want you, Sunny," I whispered, my tongue caressing her skin slowly.

"I want you too," she moaned quietly, lifting her pelvis to feel my erection as I pushed it against her.

I wanted to keep going, to take Sunny right here, right now. But I was a father and had other responsibilities, which made themselves very clear when I heard Alex call for me from his bedroom.

"Sorry," I said, trying to hide the disappointment in my voice. It was stupid to feel let down about it when I knew it wasn't like we had an opportunity to act on it anyway.

"Don't be."

I pulled away, searching her face for anything that would tell me what she was feeling right now.

She smiled, but it wasn't the one I was used to seeing. It was forced, and I was pretty sure that I could see the frustration behind it. She had already admitted that she wanted me too, but it felt good to see it and know it was genuine.

I licked my lips and then forced myself to turn around and leave. Alex was already going through his closet when I got in there, which created a nice distraction from what had just happened with Sunny.

Twenty minutes later, I had cleaned up the mess in his room and had him ready to go outside to play for a little bit. I put on a thicker pair of sweats and threw a hoodie over my long-sleeve shirt.

Sunny was adorable in her oversized sweater and sweats she had put on over her leggings and the t-shirt she wore last night. A New York Yankees beanie was pulled over her head, covering her ears. I had no idea she was a baseball fan and couldn't wait to give her shit about her team. For now, it was time to get outside and have some fun in the snow.

As soon as I opened the door, Alex took off and immediately fell into the huge pile I had cleared from in front of the sliding glass door. He was laughing hysterically as he rolled around.

"He sure loves snow," Sunny commented, rubbing her hands together in front of her face as we watched him.

"I know, it's hard to believe this is his first time playing in it."

She turned and stared at me as if I had three heads.

"What? How is that possible?"

I shrugged.

"We lived in Florida until a month ago and never got snow."

She pressed the palm of her hand to her face.

"Duh. I knew that. I swear, it's like I woke up this morning missing a handful of brain cells."

I grinned like a fool, knowing exactly why.

Before we could venture into an inappropriate conversation with Alex, I switched gears and bent down, grabbing a handful of snow and patting it into a ball.

"Alright, Buddy, you ready to build that snowman?"

We spent the next few hours rolling snow and building an entire snowman family. I didn't realize until the last minute that Alex had technically made us—me, Sunny, and him. It broke my heart a little that he didn't understand that Sunny and I weren't together, but at the same time, I felt this odd sense of relief that he was already so on board with it. That made the thought of being with her a little less scary because I didn't have to worry about how he would feel about it. But one thing that I'd learned early on in life was that if something felt like it was too good to be true, it probably was.

After we finished playing in the snow—which included a surprise snowball fight that Sunny initiated—we headed inside, and I made brunch for everyone.

Sunny and Alex sat on the couch, playing the board games she had brought over last week. I had no idea that he was old enough to really understand how games worked. Sunny assured me that it was designed for kids his age, and I was surprised by how quickly he caught on and started beating us when we all played together.

I was flipping the pancakes in the skillet when my phone

dinged with a text message. I quickly swiped it open and frowned when it was from an unknown number.

Unknown: We need to talk.

I shot off a reply about them having the wrong number and tucked my phone back into my pocket.

"Breakfast is ready," I called to them as I plated the pancakes and then set them on the table with the rest of the food.

Alex rushed down the hall to wash his hands while Sunny joined me at the table.

"Everything looks delicious. Thank you for making breakfast."

"Not a problem," I said with a smile. "I was just taking you up on your offer to *feed* you anytime. Though, I still would prefer to eat you."

I lowered my voice as I heard Alex coming down the hallway. The blush on Sunny's cheeks was beautiful, and I couldn't get enough of it.

Seventeen
Sunny

Saturday had been fun playing in the snow with Elliott and Alex, but I felt sore and achy by the evening. I helped make dinner, even though Elliott protested and insisted that he would cook for me again. It was weird how easily we fit into this couple-type vibe and acted like we were one, even though we weren't.

I was resting on the couch, desperately wanting my heat pack from my house, when Elliott decided to get Alex ready for bed. He could tell I was uncomfortable and in pain, but I didn't want to make a big deal about it. I had taken some Ibuprofen, which was as good as it would get.

"Why don't you go soak in a hot bath and see if that helps?" he offered while Alex brushed his teeth.

"Oh no, it's okay. I don't want to risk waking Alex up when I'm done."

"Use mine. I have a large soaking tub and Epsom salt. It'll help."

I pulled my brows together as I thought about it.

"Daddy, I'm ready," Alex called from his room.

He pushed up off of the couch and looked at me.

"Go start yourself a bath, or I'll do it for you once I get him down. Either way, you're soaking for a bit tonight."

He took off down the hallway before I could object.

While I wanted to fight him and insist that I was fine, my lower back said otherwise. I'd slipped on a patch of ice this morning, and even though I didn't fall, I definitely pulled something, and my body wasn't too forgiving tonight.

I went into the kitchen and poured myself a glass of wine before heading to his room.

Once I walked into the bathroom, I was stunned by how big the tub was. It was probably the largest one I had ever seen, and there was a window that looked outside so I could watch the snow falling while I soaked. Assorted candles were scattered around the tub, and a handful of jars with different scented Epsom salts. While Elliott didn't strike me as the kind of guy who took baths, I wasn't complaining about the selection of goods available to use.

I plugged the tub and then turned the water on as hot as I could stand it. While the tub filled, I sprinkled some citrus-smelling salts into the water and got undressed. I could have closed the door to give myself some privacy, but I found that I was more excited about the possibility of Elliott coming in and seeing me naked in his tub.

After last night, my body was going wild, desperate for more. I wanted to feel his fingers inside of me again as much as I wanted to ride his thick cock. Giving him a blow job was unexpected, but I loved the way he reacted to my touch and how well he fit in my mouth. I'd done my best to take all of him, but there was just too much. *Had I ever said that about a man before? He has too much cock! Nope, I didn't think so.*

The water was still filling as I climbed inside and sunk down into the warmth. It felt so good that I closed my eyes and leaned my head on the pillow attached to the tub. This was pure heaven, and I wanted to enjoy every second of it.

My mind wandered to thoughts of last night while I lifted my foot to turn off the water. I imagined it was Elliott's cock that I was touching instead and ran my toes along the cold metal. I couldn't stop obsessing over his package, even if I tried.

There was a dull aching building between my thighs as I got more and more turned on by imagining what I would do to him if I could. When he pinned me to the cabinet this morning and rubbed his erection against me, I almost came undone. Then his comment about wanting to eat me sent me even more into a frenzy.

I tilted my head to the side, imagining his lips kissing my neck again. My hands began roaming over my breasts, touching myself as I wished it was his hands instead. I opened my legs, letting the hot water rush to where I needed to be touched, and pictured Elliott's head there instead. Licking me. Sucking my clit. Fucking me with his tongue as he brought me to climax.

My fingers wrapped around a pebbled nipple while the other hand dipped below the water and started rubbing myself. I needed to come before I lost my mind. I was going crazy. Sex-crazy for Elliott and his dirty mouth.

I whimpered, my eyes still pinched shut as I envisioned him standing there, jacking off while he watched me get myself off. It was so arousing that I felt the start of my orgasm building at the same time I heard him clear his throat.

My eyes shot open, and I jerked up in the tub, splashing water over the edge as my heart raced wildly.

"Sorry, didn't mean to startle you," he said, leaning casually against the doorframe with his arms crossed over his chest. "I assumed you wanted me to come in since you left the door open."

I swallowed hard, unable to speak as we locked eyes.

"So, did you want me to catch you touching yourself, Sunny?"

I *loved* when he said my name, especially when his voice was thick with desire.

I nodded, not bothering to deny it. There was an evident bulge in his pants which meant he enjoyed what he saw.

"Show me what you like."

Now that he was here—and I knew that he was, instead of just imagining he was—I suddenly felt too nervous to do anything.

"Be a good girl and touch yourself for me, Sunny. I want to see your face as you come."

I chewed my lip nervously. There was no way I could do that.

"I can't," I said helplessly. "I'm too embarrassed."

He shook his head and walked out of the bathroom.

A few minutes later, he came back with a different toy than last night and handed it to me.

"What's this?" I asked, holding it in my hand, suddenly

nervous about him being so close to see me in my full glory.

"It's the Dark Vibes Tickler. It's waterproof and designed to suck your clit."

My cheeks flamed with heat as I studied the hot pink toy in my hands.

"Go ahead, try it out. I'll step out and let you enjoy yourself this time—but next time, I get to watch."

He stepped out and pulled the door closed behind him, leaving me a flustered, wet mess.

Next time? He was already planning on there being a next time?

I studied the device and flipped it over before giving in and sliding it inside of me. It fit snuggly and went surprisingly deep while the flower part pressed firmly against my clit. I pressed the button to turn it on and jumped at the intensity as the whole toy vibrated.

It wasn't painful or uncomfortable, just a bit overwhelming at first. I leaned back against the pillow and closed my eyes while I got used to the sensation.

A few minutes later, I gripped the side of the tub as I kept from screaming as another intense orgasm came rushing over me.

Water sloshed over the sides of the tub again, making a mess I would have to clean up once I was done, but I couldn't care about that right now. I was too busy obsessing over how my body felt as I pulled the toy out and set it on the edge of the tub beside me.

Even though I didn't know Elliott as well as I wanted to, the one thing that I knew for sure was that he had some fantastic toys, and I couldn't wait to save up so I could get some of my own.

Eighteen
Elliott

I was leaning against the headboard when Sunny came out of the bathroom. While I desperately wanted to watch her get herself off in my bathtub, I would never push her to do something she wasn't comfortable with.

When I heard her soft moans float through underneath the door, I knew she had tried the toy I'd given her. I was so turned on that I decided to change out of my jeans and into sweats so my dick wouldn't feel like it would explode.

"Did you enjoy your soak?" I asked casually as she emerged, wearing nothing but a bath towel wrapped around her body.

Fuuuccckkk. I wanted to rip it off of her and finally have my way with her.

"It was wonderful, thank you. I'm jealous of your tub and wish mine was that big."

"I'm glad the size of my tub impresses you," I chuckled.

"Well, size does matter."

She was chewing her lip again, the way she did when she was feeling flustered. I loved that about her.

"Oh, does it?"

She nodded.

"Well, then, how do I stack up?" I got off the bed and walked over to where she was standing.

She tilted her head to look at me, and I could see the desire in her eyes.

"Very well. Everything I've seen so far exceeds expectations."

Her breathing changed, making her voice raspier.

"Good to know."

We were standing toe to toe, my fingers itching to reach out and relieve her of the towel so I could touch her body.

Without thinking it through, I lifted her chin with my finger and lowered my lips to hers.

She raised her arms, wrapping them around my neck as she deepened the kiss.

I walked her backward to my bed, lifting her to my hips as soon as we reached it. We hadn't talked about how far things would go between us, but then again, neither of us was doing much to stop this.

When she locked her legs around my waist and tried to dry hump me, I didn't have to guess what she wanted.

"Fuck me, Elliott," she panted as she broke the kiss and looked at me. "I know we're not supposed to, but I don't care if you don't. Please. Just fuck me. I need to feel you inside of me. Pleeeasse—"

I covered her mouth with mine, swallowing her words as she begged me to do what I had been wanting to do to her.

I dropped her onto the bed, earning a giggle as she flopped down. She stared at me as she unhooked her towel and opened it, leaving her completely naked and spread eagle when she spread her legs for me.

"There are so many things I want to do to you, Sunny," I said as I climbed onto the bed and pulled a hardened nipple into my mouth.

"Do them. All of them." She moaned deeply, instantly making my dick even harder.

Suddenly I remembered that I hadn't locked my bedroom door so I got up and rushed over to lock it.

"Good call," she laughed, lying back down as I pulled my t-shirt off and tossed it across the room.

"I also brought in the baby monitor, so we'll hear if he gets up."

She winked in agreement, looking ridiculously sexy. I stripped off the rest of my clothes and climbed up next to her.

I wanted to take my time worshipping her body, but my cock reminded me that it needed a release sooner than later and that I needed to get the party started already.

"What do you like, Sunny?" I asked as I rolled on top of her, kissing the side of her neck while my hands eagerly roamed over her body.

"Whatever you want," she panted, scratching her nails down my back as I slipped a finger inside her. "That, I like that."

"Mmm, good girl. What else do you like? How do you want me to fuck you?"

I pushed another finger in and pumped harder, loving how she gripped me in response.

"Ahhhh. Yes. Yes. YES!"

"Shhh, we have to be quiet, baby. Tell me how you want it."

"However you want it."

I paused and pulled my fingers out.

Her eyes narrowed as she stared at me.

"When I ask how you want something, I need you to tell me. Don't be passive in bed, Sunny. Demand what you want. Tell me how you want to be touched, how you want to be fucked."

She blushed slightly and looked away.

"Sunny," I warned, hoping she would talk to me so we could get back to the good stuff.

"I don't know," she said with a heavy sigh. "I've only done it the basic way. It's not like I have all of these sexy things I've done or know what I like because I haven't tried much."

"Fuck," I muttered under my breath, forgetting again just how young she was. "I'm sorry, I didn't think about that."

"It's okay. I wasn't one of those girls who did it a lot. I haven't had many boyfriends, and I'm not usually someone who sleeps with guys I'm not dating."

I pulled my brows together and studied her.

"Sunny, are you sure you want to do this?"

We weren't dating, and I didn't want this to be something she would later regret.

"Yes. I'm positive. I don't care that we're not dating, Elliott. I don't know what that means, I just know that I've never felt this way with anyone before, and I'm seriously two seconds away from humping your pillow because I'm that wound up right now."

My head fell back as a deep laugh rumbled out of me.

"Not that I wouldn't enjoy seeing you hump my pillow, but I'd rather that you didn't. If you want to ride something, I've got plenty of options for you."

Her green eyes sparkled as she popped up on her elbows.

"Oh yeah, like what?"

"My face, cock, or fingers. Ladies' choice."

I'd never seen anyone's cheeks get as red as hers did.

"What's wrong?" I asked, enjoying every second of this. "Cat got your tongue?"

She looked around as if someone else might hear us and then whispered.

"I can't ride your face."

I rolled over onto my back and turned my head to look at her.

"Why not?"

"Because! I just can't!"

"You can and you will."

She was now sitting up, attempting to cover her breasts with her arm as she stared at me in disbelief.

I reached over and grabbed her hand, yanking until she was beside me. Once I could get a good grip on her, I swung her onto my body, so she was straddling my waist. If she scooted down just a little bit, she could ride my cock. If I scooted down, she could ride my face. Either way, she was about to ride something.

I gripped her hips, holding her in place so she couldn't get away.

"Elliott, I'm not going to sit on your face."

"I don't see what the problem is."

"You won't be able to breathe! You'll suffocate!"

"Trust me, I won't," I assured her. "But if I do, that would be a fucking amazing way to go."

She shook her head and looked away for a moment while I took the opportunity to get into position. She squirmed and giggled as I slid and then lifted her, so her pussy was right over my mouth. I could smell the scent of the Epsom salts she used and couldn't wait to taste her.

"Elliott, no, stop," she objected as she tried to move away.

I gripped her thighs even tighter, holding her in place as I started to lick her.

She stopped moving once she felt my tongue in between

her folds, and I could feel her body relax. She lasted a few minutes before her legs started to tremble from trying to hold herself above me instead of just sitting like I wanted her to.

I stopped what I was doing and looked up at her.

"Sunny—"

"Yeah?"

"Sit on my fucking face."

I pinned her with a look that said I wasn't playing, and she finally allowed herself to relax against me. Once I didn't have to fight her anymore, I rubbed my hands up her thighs and continued eating her out. I felt her tighten around me and knew that she was getting close.

This time I wanted her to have the orgasm as it was approaching instead of all of the interrupted ones she'd had recently. I focused on her clit, sucking hard until I heard her whimpering my name and knew she was coming.

Once she was done, I didn't rush her to get down. I wanted her to feel comfortable there and to know that I enjoyed this position more than anything. I loved having a woman ride my face and use me to get off.

She let out a heavy sigh and slowly started scooting down my body, leaving a trail of wetness behind.

Her hand reached down and grabbed my cock, gripping it hard before she began stroking it.

"I want to ride this next," she said softly, nipping my ear.

"It's all yours, baby. There are condoms in the top drawer

of the nightstand.”

She leaned over and grabbed one, then handed it to me as she rolled off so I could put it on. Once I was covered, I laid back and put my arms behind my head as she climbed on top.

I watched in awe as she slowly slid down, holding my dick in her hand as she lined herself up. As soon as I was fully seated inside her, she moved her hips and began grinding against me.

The way I fit inside her was unlike anything I’d ever felt. She was so fucking tight that it made it feel that much more intense. I couldn’t even begin to imagine how fucking good it would feel to fuck her without a condom, but for now, we needed to be safe.

She rocked back and forth, closing her eyes as she enjoyed touching her breasts and rolling her nipples between her fingers. It was a gorgeous sight to see Sunny touch herself, just like it was to watch her come undone.

I liked the slow and steady way she was riding me, but I also wanted to pound into her and give her the best sex of her life. As if reading my thoughts, she opened her eyes and smiled down at me.

“I want you to fuck me the way you want to, Elliott. Don’t be gentle; just fuck me. Hard. Fast. I want it.”

Without needing any additional approval, I lifted her off me and then quickly flipped her over so she was on her hands and knees. I lined up at her entrance and pushed inside, loving how she cried out my name.

Taking her from behind allowed me to watch her ass as it

bounced the harder I plunged into her. She bent forward and tried to muffle her moans into the pillow as I went deeper and faster.

Soon, I was releasing inside of the condom, feeling the way her pussy wrapped around me as she came again.

124

Nineteen

Sunny

I'd spent another week at Elliott's even though the storm had finally stopped, and it was safe to go home. For whatever reason, we couldn't seem to get enough of each other, and I'd gone from sleeping on the couch to sleeping in his bed and slipping out each morning before Alex woke up. We also couldn't keep our hands off each other, and even though we had fun with the toys we used, nothing could top the amazing, mind-blowing sex we had—which seemed to be an every night thing lately.

Though, I had followed through on my promise to try out the new toy and report my findings back to him. Knowing how much he enjoyed watching me touch myself, I'd taken my time soaking again in his giant tub and tried the toy while he sat in the corner of the bathroom and jacked off as he watched me play with myself. The toy was just as fabulous as the others, so it was hard to decide whether I had a favorite. But to make sure I was giving adequate feedback on it, we tried it out three more times after that, and Elliott reported back to his team that it was definitely meeting expectations.

It was a week until Christmas, and we were spending the weekend together doing *family* stuff, like finishing up our Christmas shopping and going to the Frosty Fest parade this morning. While Saturday mornings used to be my downtime to sit and relax, I found that I preferred waking up early and spending time with them instead.

I knew it would be cold at the parade, but it was their first year spending the holidays in Sugarplum Falls, and I wanted them to experience everything the town had to offer. The festival officially started after the parade, and we had already planned to take Alex to see Santa before doing some shopping at the mall.

Elliott and I got up early and enjoyed our morning coffee together while Alex slept. The parade didn't start until nine, so we had plenty of time before then. Once I heard Alex was up, I excused myself to go shower and get ready.

"I left something I want you to wear today," Elliott whispered in my ear as we passed each other. "It's on the counter in the bathroom."

"Okay," I said with a smile, curious to see what it was.

I went inside and locked the door before turning on the shower and stripping off my clothes.

Lying beside the sink was a box with a small vibrator inside. I read the outside of the package and found that it was discreet enough to wear in my panties and that there was an app that you could use to control it—which I assumed would be Elliott's job.

I shook my head and sighed as I climbed into the shower and got ready for a day of beautiful torture.

Once we got to the parade, we found a spot toward the beginning. We had Alex stand in front of us while we stood behind him. It was cold, but we'd dressed for it and made sure Alex was bundled up, so he didn't get cranky.

The parade started, and we watched as the different floats went by and the town locals waved and tossed candy canes into the audience. I was getting colder when all of a sudden, I felt a buzzing in my panties.

My head whipped up to look at Elliott, who was watching the parade as if nothing had happened. His hands were inside the pockets of his peacoat, making it hard for me to see where his phone was or how he was doing it.

"There's a remote control," he whispered out of the side of his mouth while I continued to look ahead and wave at the kids from the marching band.

"You can't be serious, you want to do this *here*?" I whispered back.

"Why not? You looked cold, so I thought I would help warm you up."

He pressed a button and the intensity amplified.

I bit my lip to keep from crying out as I scanned the crowd around us to make sure no one knew what was happening.

Jasmin, the woman who runs everything with the Frosty Fest, including the parade, was standing beside me when I accidentally let out a small gasp.

Her head whipped in my direction, looking for the problem.

"One of the band kids almost fell," I lied and pointed in their direction to get her attention away from me.

I could hear Elliott chuckle beside me.

I was trying to focus on anything other than the pleasure pulsing through my panties and sending heat waves crashing over my body.

I tried to smile back at Andi as she rode on the Sugarplum Sweets float and had kids dressed as elves that tossed wrapped caramels from her store at everyone. I knew I looked awkward when she frowned, then looked at Elliott, who was pretending like nothing was happening as he looked away. I'd known Andi since we were kids and had a lot of the same classes together. While I wouldn't say we were best friends, she was the one I confided in and shared all of my secrets with.

I hadn't caught her up on what was going on between Elliott and me, but I could tell by the smirk that was now gracing her lips that she was figuring it out on her own. She shook her finger at me playfully, then turned her attention to the other side of the street before anyone noticed who she had done it to.

The next few floats that passed by were a blur as Elliott increased the pulsating vibrations and nearly sent me over the edge.

I barely had a chance to see that Santa and Mrs. Claus were heading our way when he pushed it up higher. I squeezed my legs together and reached down to grab his hand. My nails dug into his skin as I gripped him tightly while quietly trying to ride out my orgasm.

"YES!!" I squealed accidentally, my eyes widening in horror as Jasmin and a few other people turned to look at me.

Elliott turned his head and coughed, trying to disguise his laughter. I let go of his hand and tried to compose myself.

Everyone else had already turned around, but Jasmin's attention was still on me.

"Sorry," I laughed nervously. "I just get excited when Santa and Mrs. Claus come out."

"Don't be," she said happily, adjusting to face me head-on. "I love your enthusiasm. You should sign up next year to be in the parade. So often, we have people who just sit there and wave, faking it. Sugarplum Falls prides itself on its Christmas spirit, and girl, you've definitely got it!"

"Oh, I don't know about that," I replied quickly, feeling the heat from Elliott's body as he turned into me.

"Come on, you'd be perfect! That was a genuine reaction you had. I can't say that I've ever had that with anyone who's been in the parade before. You'd make an excellent elf!"

"Trust me, Sunny never fakes it," Elliott said with a cheeky smile right before I elbowed him in the ribs.

Twenty
Elliott

The day flew by, and before I knew it, I was carrying armloads of shopping bags into the house and wondering how I got suckered into spending so much. I'd already done most of my shopping for Alex and had a few gifts picked out for Sunny, but today was different. It was fun going through the stores with them and picking out things as *a family*. Or at least that's what it felt like and it was messing with my head.

I set them down on the table and let Sunny and Alex unpack them while I started dinner. Sunny had offered to cook, but I found that I enjoyed the way she moaned quietly when she ate the food I made, so I was technically planning to cook for her for the rest of our lives.

The ground beef sizzled in the pan while they laughed at the robot cookie jars we'd bought that were dressed like Santa and Mrs. Claus. They were cute, but I wasn't big on sweets, so I didn't see a need for them. Sunny, on the other hand, insisted that *everyone* needed some treats during the holidays and stocked us up on enough cookies and candies to give all of us diabetes.

I worked on washing the lettuce and tomato while the meat cooked and the taco shells warmed in the oven. It was a simple dinner, and if I were being honest, I would rather eat

Sunny's taco than the ones I was cooking. Not that there was anything wrong with the food I made, I just couldn't get enough of eating her out. It was like a new obsession that I never knew I had.

"Which cookies do you want to put in this one?" Sunny asked, holding up the Santa robot.

"Those ones!" Alex said excitedly, pointing to the chocolate chip cookies.

"Okay, and which ones for this one?"

He tapped his chin with his finger as he thought about it.

"Oreos!"

"You got it!"

She squeezed in beside me, allowing her body to brush against mine as she washed the cookie jars.

"Do I get to eat your cookie later?" I asked quietly so only she could hear.

"Why, Mr. Weston, I thought you'd never ask," she teased, batting her long, dark eyelashes at me. "Besides, you owe me from earlier."

"What are you referring to, Ms. Wells?" I stirred the ground beef and added some taco seasoning.

"The incident at the parade."

"What?" I laughed. "I wasn't lying—you don't fake it."

"I still can't believe you did that."

She shook her head as she washed the other robot,

forgetting that Alex was still in the room at the kitchen table.

"What did he do?"

Sunny froze and gave me a panicked look, refusing to turn around and look at him.

"I farted." I turned to find him with a goofy grin as he tried to cover his mouth with his hand.

"Eeewww, Dad!"

"Right? It was so gross," Sunny added, giving me a pointed look even though I had just saved her butt.

"Sorry, I thought I could blame it on the reindeer. We all know how much they fart. It wouldn't be that far-fetched."

"The reindeer were sooooo cool," Alex gushed, already over my made-up story.

"I loved petting them," Sunny said, taking the cookie jars over to the table and letting Alex help her fill them.

"That one tried to bite me," I added, remembering how I had to back away when it kept leaning forward and nipping at my crotch.

"He was just looking for a carrot." Sunny chewed her lip and locked eyes with me, sharing another private moment.

"Well, like I told him, I don't carry carrots with me. I only pack thick eggplant."

I turned back to the tacos and ignored my son's confused look, likely wondering where I would store an eggplant.

After dinner, I gave Alex a bath while Sunny soaked in

my tub. I couldn't wait to spend more time with her, even though we had technically spent the entire day together, I couldn't wait for one-on-one adult time with her.

Once Alex was down, I turned on the baby monitor and sat in bed, browsing social media on my phone while Sunny finished soaking. I had been getting messages from the same unknown number all week and frowned when another one came through.

Unknown: You can't avoid me forever. I will find you and we will talk.

I wanted to reply and tell them to leave me the fuck alone, but it was useless. I'd already paid to have someone trace the number, but it came back as a burner phone with no leads on who had purchased it.

The frown was still etched on my face when Sunny came out, wearing a towel wrapped around her body.

"What's wrong?" she asked, sitting on the bed next to me.

"Nothing," I lied, setting the phone on the nightstand.

"You're a terrible liar. You do know that, right?"

I rolled my eyes and pulled her closer to me, tugging her towel loose in the process.

"I've been getting text messages from an unknown number for a week, and it's starting to drive me crazy."

"What kind of messages?" she asked, looking up at me.

"Dirty ones. Naked pictures."

She whipped away from me so fast that I couldn't keep my hands around her.

"What?" Her eyes looked like they were going to pop out of her head.

"Relax," I laughed. "I'm just kidding. They're not dirty, and there have been no pictures."

I grabbed my phone, unlocked it, then handed it to her so she could read through them.

She eyed me suspiciously before taking it.

"But, if you ever want to change that, I wouldn't mind you sending me some."

She reached over and shoved me, allowing me to grab her again. I pulled her closer and kissed the side of her head before putting my phone back on the nightstand.

"I'm not that kind of girl."

"Fair enough. I'd rather have you naked in the flesh than a picture anyway."

"Yeah?"

"Yup."

"Why's that?"

"Because I can't eat a picture out, Sunny."

She giggled as I slid down next to her and positioned myself between her legs. I didn't have to fight her for access anymore—which I loved. It was like we were so perfect for each other that everything was easy, and we just went with the flow. I loved that there was no drama or tension between us—other than the sexual tension when we had to keep our hands off each other when Alex was awake. Other than that, nothing to worry about, and I loved it.

I continued to torture her with my tongue, teasing her pussy as I licked and sucked, gently nibbling when I could. Before I knew it, her body shook as her pussy spasmed around me, and my name floated off her tongue like a curse word.

After she came, I held her in my arms, not feeling the rush to be inside of her. It was still early, and I knew we would have plenty of time for that later. She seemed tired, and I wanted nothing more than just to cuddle and relax.

"What are your plans for Christmas?" I asked nervously. We'd spent so much time together lately that I couldn't imagine her going home again, but I also couldn't ignore that she likely had family that she would be spending the day with.

"I don't have any," she said quietly, resting her head on my chest.

"Are you spending it with your family?"

"I don't really have any family here anymore. My sister lives in New York, and my mom is on a cruise with her new boyfriend, so it's just me."

I remembered her talking about her dad not being here anymore, so I didn't push about whether she was okay with not spending this year with her family. The last thing I wanted to do was bring up sad memories or make her feel bad.

"Do you want to spend Christmas with Alex and me?" I asked, rubbing my hands up and down her arms soothingly.

She froze beneath my touch, and I started to panic that she was going to say no.

"You don't have to do that," she said quietly, not looking back at me.

I leaned around the side and positioned myself so that I could see her face.

"I know I don't *have* to. I want to. Alex and I would really enjoy having you spend the day with us."

"I don't know," she said as she nervously chewed her nail.

"Why not?"

"Because I don't want it to get confusing for him."

"What do you mean?"

"I think we've already pushed the boundaries with me staying here for so long. What is he going to think if I'm here for Christmas too?"

"He'll think that you enjoy spending time with us as much as we enjoy spending time with you and that we're all celebrating the holiday together."

"Yeah, but what if he starts to think that I should be there for every holiday or that I'm part of the fa—"

"Family?" I finished for her.

She snapped her mouth shut and looked away.

"Would it be so bad if he did?"

I could feel the tension tightening the muscles in her shoulders, and I hated it.

"I don't know."

I leaned back and shoved a hand through my hair. I wasn't

planning to have this conversation with her right now, but it seemed like it was going to happen regardless.

"Look, Sunny, I don't know what the future holds or where things will go between us, but I do know that both Alex and I are the happiest we've ever been, and that's because of you. If you're not ready to consider yourself part of our family, that's fine. But that doesn't mean we don't love you like you are."

Her head whipped around, the shock on her face at my dropping the L word matching my own. But the weird thing was that I didn't regret it, nor did I try to backtrack and pretend like I hadn't said it.

"I love you, Sunny. I know that I shouldn't and that you're too young for me, but I don't care. There are a million reasons why we shouldn't be together, but I'm only focusing on the reasons why we belong together. Nothing you say is going to change that."

She lifted a finger and wiped the wetness from the corner of her eyes.

"I love you too," she said softly, allowing me to pull her into my chest again.

"So, does that mean you'll spend Christmas with us?"

She nodded and giggled when I tickled her sides.

"I need to hear you say it," I warned, digging my fingers in deeper.

"Yes!" she squealed. "Yes!"

"That's my girl." I smiled cockily as I rolled her onto her back and made love to the woman who brought out the best in me and just made me the happiest man in the world by saying she loved me too.

Twenty-One
Sunny

I was flipping pancakes when Elliott came up behind me, wrapped an arm around my waist, and then slipped his other hand down the front of my sweats and dipped a finger between my folds.

"Elliott!" I scolded, checking over my shoulder to make sure Alex wasn't there.

"Don't worry; he's still sleeping. I just checked. Plus, I closed his door so we'll hear him when he comes out."

"You're a naughty, naughty man," I teased as he continued to finger me, pushing in and out as I tried not to burn the food.

"You know you like it," he growled deep in my ear.

"True, but you're not going to like it if I burn breakfast."

"Good point."

He pulled his hand out and I immediately missed it. Then he reached around me, turned off the burner, and moved the skillet to the back of the stove.

"There, problem solved."

"What are you doing?" I laughed as he pulled my pants and panties down.

"Having breakfast."

He lifted me up and placed me on the counter with my back facing the hallway.

"Now be a good girl and I'll let you come on my face. But we gotta be quick before Alex wakes up."

Before I could say anything, he pushed me back and lowered his mouth to my pussy, where he started licking and sucking.

We weren't going to have a problem with being quick at this rate. My body was already used to his touch, and he knew me well enough now to know how to get me off quickly. He inserted two fingers inside me, pumping hard and fast while he sucked my clit.

Within minutes, I was coming and biting my lip to keep from screaming. We heard a noise down the hall so Elliott helped me down and pulled my pants up just in time before Alex came walking down the hallway.

I tried to act normal as I grabbed the skillet and moved it back to the burner.

"Good morning, Buddy," Elliott said, taking a seat at the table. I could feel his eyes on me and knew that he was probably hard as a rock right now. I wanted nothing more than to return the favor, but it would have to wait until tonight when Alex was in bed. It was weird but oddly satisfying that we had such a rigid sex schedule, but I guess that's what you did when you had kids.

"Good morning," he replied sleepily.

"How did you sleep?" Elliott asked, lifting his coffee mug to his lips.

I smiled at Alex and then turned back to the pancakes, noticing that I'd forgotten to turn the burner back on. Apparently, I was more distracted than I thought.

"Okay. My tummy hurts."

"Are you okay?"

"Yeah, I probably just have to poop."

I laughed at the stove and turned the pancakes, even though they didn't need it yet. That kid sure loved to talk about poop and honestly believed it was the cure-all whenever someone complained of a stomach ache.

While they talked, I finished making breakfast and set it on the table. I was grabbing the juice from the fridge when we heard the doorbell ring.

I looked at Elliott, who looked at me and then shrugged. He got up and opened the door, letting in a blast of cold air.

"What the hell are you doing here?"

I frowned and set the juice on the table before going over to see what the problem was.

A beautiful woman was standing on the other side wearing a fitted red dress and a fur coat that screamed expensive. I had never seen her before, but when she took her designer sunglasses off, I recognized the familiar blue eyes from the photo in Alex's room.

"I'm back."

BLAME IT ON THE EGGNOG

Twenty-Two

Elliott

"What are you doing here, Sharon?" My teeth were gritted tightly as I stared at her. I could feel Sunny behind me and knew she would quickly put the pieces together.

"I've been messaging you, but like always, you refuse to respond. It seems you left me no choice but to just show up."

"Well, maybe if you would have said who it was in the message, you would have gotten a better response."

I was still standing at the door, blocking her from coming in any further.

"Like you would have talked to me," she scoffed.

"So instead, you just show up, a week before Christmas, and demand that I talk to you? There's nothing to talk about. Everything was said during the divorce. You got what you wanted. So why are you here?"

"I didn't get everything," she said quietly, looking past me to Sunny.

Before I could stop it, Alex came flying around the corner into the entryway and looked up at her.

I wasn't sure whether he would recognize Sharon, given

that she'd been gone from his life for the past two years. But the moment he saw her, he flung himself into her arms as she bent down to hug him.

"Mom!"

I swallowed hard, trying to get rid of the bile that was threatening to come out.

"I'm going to go," Sunny said, gently grabbing my arm to get my attention.

"No, please don't."

"It's okay. You guys obviously have stuff to talk about. Plus, I need to get home."

"Yes, we do have *stuff* to talk about," Sharon said coldly, eyeing Sunny. "And it's a *private family matter*."

"Yes, of course." Sunny lowered her head and then headed to my bedroom to grab her stuff.

"Are you going to have breakfast with us?" Alex asked, leading her in by her hand.

"Umm, sure, I'd love to," she replied, challenging me with a look.

"Unfortunately, your mom is just here to talk to me for a few minutes, Buddy. I don't think she's going to be able to stay long." I spoke to Alex but kept my eyes locked on Sharon, making sure she was getting my point loud and clear.

"But she just got here," Alex pouted.

"Yeah, Elliott, I just got here."

I hated that she used her own child to try to manipulate me.

A few minutes later, Sunny came down the hallway with bags full of her stuff, looking frazzled.

"Are you leaving too?" Alex asked, tears starting to well in his eyes.

Sunny squatted in front of him and gently brushed them away with her thumb.

"Yeah, I need to go home and take care of a few things. But I'll be back in the morning, and we'll make sprinkle pancakes, okay?"

"Okay."

He climbed up in his chair and started eating his breakfast again while the adults had a conversation I never wanted to have again.

"*Why* is she coming back in the morning?" Sharon narrowed her eyes at Sunny, who lowered her head again.

"Because she's his nanny and because we *actually* want her here."

"Well then, we should let *the help* be on their way."

I could see the tears in Sunny's eyes and wanted to hold her and tell her it would be okay.

She turned and headed to the door as I followed right behind her.

"Sunny, please, let me explain."

"Explain what, Elliott? It's not like you knew she was coming. There's nothing to explain."

"Still, it doesn't mean that I want you to leave or that I'm okay with you being upset. She's a terrible person, Sunny—that's why I divorced her."

"It's fine, really. Alex is excited to see her, and that's all that matters."

"Sunny—"

She opened the door and walked out before I could say anything else.

My blood was boiling by the time I went into the kitchen with Sharon and Alex. They were sitting together at the table while she pretended to be interested in what he was saying. She was almost as fake as her boobs that had grown a size or two since I'd last seen her.

"And then—the reindeer farted!" Alex laughed.

Sharon tossed her head back and laughed, exposing her slender neck that I wanted to wrap my hands around and strangle.

"Alex, please finish your breakfast and then you can go watch your show in the living room. Your mother and I need to talk."

"Okay, daddy."

I nodded my head for Sharon to follow me and then realized there wasn't a single part of my house I wanted her to be in. I didn't want her to see any of it and it was bad enough that she had already found out where we lived.

I led her back to the entryway and lowered my voice so Alex couldn't hear us.

"Why are you here?"

"Aww, are you going to pretend you didn't miss me?"

"No. I'm dead serious when I say that I didn't. Why. Are. You. Here?"

"I wanted to see Alex. It's Christmas, and I'm his mom. I should get to spend the holiday with him."

"You gave up that right when you took the house in Florida and my dog. What's the real reason, Sharon? Cut the bullshit."

"Fine," she sighed, pushing her sunglasses onto her head. It was ridiculous that she was wearing them, given we were still sitting on a blanket of snow, but I assumed she needed them when she left Florida and must've come straight here.

"Spit it out."

"I *heard* that you were doing really well with your business, and I realized that I hadn't been a very supportive wife before, so I wanted to rectify that now."

"Or you heard that I was doing well, and you came back thinking you'd get more money."

I knew that her brother-in-law still worked for me, but he seemed to like her even less than I did, so I never worried about him leaking information. That was another problem I'd need to deal with, which I hated because I used to like Stan.

"What?" She pulled her head back, gasped, and clutched a hand to her chest. Her performance was so dramatic that she could have passed for one of those women on the cheesy soap operas I sometimes watched with my mom growing up.

"Really?" I questioned with one eyebrow raised and my arms folded over my chest.

"Fine. Whatever." She waved her hand dismissively at me. "But you can't say that you're not curious about what could happen between us, Elliott. There was a time when we were happy and in love. And we have a child together. A child that deserves to have a happy family. Don't shut me out of his life just because you're still mad at me. Give me a chance to fix things."

"No."

"Elliott!"

"No, Sharon. You made it clear what you wanted when you walked out. You made it clear what you wanted when you demanded all of the expensive stuff in the divorce. Don't you dare come in here pretending to be a caring mother. If you want to be a good mother, then leave and don't ever come back."

"I can't believe you have the balls to say that to me."

"Don't act like you know anything about my balls."

"Well, I'm sure that *girl* does."

I picked up on the jealousy in her voice and enjoyed every tiny bit of it.

"That girl is *none* of your business."

"No, but you are."

"Wrong again. I don't have time for this, Sharon. I'm going to make myself very clear—I have no interest in starting anything up with you again. You got everything you are going to get from me in the divorce. If you show up here again, using your son to get something from me, I will file a restraining order and have your ass thrown in jail for harassment."

"You can't do that!" She gasped loud enough for Alex to hear before he came down the hallway to check on us.

I pointed in his direction and shook my head, sending him back to the kitchen.

"Don't try me, Sharon."

"I just want a chance, Elliott. Come on, it's Christmas, and I've learned from my mistakes."

"And yet you came here because a little birdie told you I was doing well financially. This sounds like a repeat pattern to me."

She lowered her head as if she was ashamed, but that would mean that she would have to be a human capable of emotion—which she wasn't.

"Please, Elliott."

"It's time for you to go."

I opened the door and stepped to the side, waiting for her to leave.

"Don't I get to say goodbye to Alex?"

Part of me wanted to say no, that she forfeited that right the first time she walked away from him, but I wasn't a cold-hearted monster.

"Make it quick."

She took off to the kitchen, and I heard them talking before she came back and blinked the tears away. She opened her mouth to say something but snapped it shut when she saw my jaw clenched. As soon as she was out of the way, I slammed the door and locked it.

I pulled my phone out of my pocket and dialed the HR manager's cell phone number.

"Hello, Elliott," she greeted, not questioning why I was calling on a Sunday.

"Hello, Jane. I need you to process the paperwork to terminate employment for Stan Hughes immediately. I'll send an email shortly with an explanation for you."

"Yes, sir. I'll take care of it."

I hung up feeling better to have taken care of one problem. Now I had what felt like a million others staring at me, like a little boy in the kitchen that I would have to go let down when I told him that his mother had left again and wouldn't be back.

Twenty-Three
Sunny

I had avoided Elliott's calls and text messages all day yesterday and felt terrible for calling in this morning. I knew that it would be upsetting to Alex that I broke my promise of being there, but honestly, I was in no condition to be around them right now.

My head hurt from overthinking everything last night as I cried my sorrows into a carton of ice cream and drank Moscato straight out of the bottle. It boggled my mind how it could go so quickly from Elliott telling me he loved me to having his ex-wife show up, wanting to be in their lives again.

Even though Elliott assured me through numerous texts and voicemails that he had no plans of giving her another chance, it didn't settle the nagging feeling in my stomach that told me I needed to back off and leave them be. Alex deserved to have both of his parents in his life if there was a way, and I wasn't going to be the thing that stood in the way.

I'd made sure to make arrangements for them this morning and asked Beverly to cover for me. She was a few years younger than I was, but she was an excellent babysitter and would do amazing with Alex. I didn't give Elliott a choice in the matter, just told him that she would be there by eight and that I was sorry for the last-minute change.

Since then, I'd been curled up on my couch, feeling sorry for myself as I watched sappy romantic movies on TV that just furthered my depression.

My phone dinged with a text message, and I didn't bother reaching for it, knowing it was Elliott again. Then another one came through. And another.

Finally, I sighed and grabbed it from the coffee table.

Andi: What's going on? Beverly said she was covering for you today at the Weston house and I know it's not like you to miss work.

Andi: Are you sick? Do you need some soup? Or maybe some peppermint bark?

Andi: Okay, I'm officially starting to worry about you. If you don't answer me, I'm coming over and bringing everything peppermint with me. It'll be a pepper-vention. Get it? Like an intervention but with peppermint?

Andi: Forget it. I'm on my way.

I didn't have the energy to respond and didn't bother since I knew it was too late. She would be there in a few—yup, there she was.

I got up and wrapped the blanket around my shoulders, unable to get warm, as I opened the door and moved to the side to let her in.

"Okay, spill it. What happened?"

She handed me a cup of coffee, and I took it, not bothering to ask what was in it. I closed the door and went back to the couch while she set her purse down and carried a tray full of baked goods over with her. She sat down beside me and waited for me to talk while she sipped her coffee.

"Nothing happened," I lied, taking a sip.

The drink was hot, but it was the insane amount of alcohol in it that burned my throat more.

"Fuck, Andi! What the hell is in this?"

"I had Sam slip something special into your drink; I figured you could use it this morning."

"Sam from Sugarplum Lattes? The nicest guy in town has a secret stash of booze?"

She shrugged like it was no big deal—which, honestly, I couldn't say it was. It was potent but tasted delicious after I got used to the initial burn.

"His coffee shop is literally next door to Sugar Face Bar. I'm sure they swap drinks all the time," she laughed.

"Very true," I laughed.

"Okay, so tell me what's going on. Why did you miss work today?"

"It's not a big deal." I shrugged. "I was feeling a little under the weather. People are allowed to call in when they're sick, Andi."

She tilted her head to the side and studied me as she lifted her cup to her lips.

"Yeah, but you're not sick."

I sipped my coffee slowly, avoiding the look she was giving me.

"Come on, Sunny. We tell each other everything. Something is going on, and I'm genuinely worried about you. You're not the bright, happy girl I'm used to seeing. I can literally feel the sadness rolling off of you, and it's making me sad. Talk to me. What happened with Elliott?"

I pulled the blanket up closer to my chin and curled into it.

"What makes you think something happened with him?"

"Oh, please. It's obvious something was going on between the two of you. I could tell from the moment I saw you guys together at the cookie decorating event when you turned poor Santa into some jizz-covered eroticookie."

"That's not a word," I muttered as I tried to fight back a grin.

"No, but it's going to be." She wiggled her eyebrows. "Thanks to you guys and your suggestion, I'm going to offer some couples cookie decorating classes in the new year. I'm thinking about starting around Valentine's Day and having the couples bake the cookies together so they can get their hands dirty as they mix the dough and—"

"Okay, okay," I laughed. "I don't need the dirty details."

"You're right. It seems you're already way ahead of me with the eroticookie thing anyway."

Images of Elliott and me over the last few weeks rushed through my mind, forcing me to pinch my eyes closed as I tried to ignore them.

"So, what happened?"

I opened my eyes and blinked away the tears as I looked at her.

"I fell for him. Hard."

She smiled softly.

"He doesn't feel the same way?"

I shrugged and took another sip.

"I think he does. He told me he loved me for the first time yesterday."

"And what did you say?"

I looked up at her and felt a tear slip down my face.

"I told him I loved him too."

She frowned, confused by what the problem was.

"And then his ex-wife showed up and asked for another chance. Alex was so excited to see her, Andi. Watching it broke my heart, and I knew I had to leave. I can't stand in the way of him being able to have his mom in his life."

"Does Elliott want to get back together with her?"

"I don't know," I sighed heavily. "He's been texting and calling since yesterday, but I haven't talked to him. He says he's not getting back together with her, but that doesn't mean I should be with him."

"Why not?"

"Because it's not fair to Alex. I grew up not having my father, and I know how hard that is. Alex has a chance to have both of his parents in his life. I refuse to be the reason he doesn't. I have to walk away, Andi. It's the only way he's going to be happy."

"But what about Elliott? It's not fair to him that he doesn't get to be with you."

I lifted my shoulders and let them fall with my tears.

"That's the thing about love. It's not always fair. I love them both enough to want the best for them."

Andi lifted her coffee to her lips and took a drink. Neither of us bothered to say anything more. We just sat there and drank our spiked coffee as I prayed it would numb the pain inside.

Twenty-Four
Elliott

Alex had the Christmas music up louder than I'd like and was singing along with the kids on TV while all I could think was fa la la la la, fuck it all.

It had been three days since Sunny walked out and left, and the knot in my stomach had only increased since then. I spent all day Sunday trying to get her to talk to me without any luck. By Monday, she'd finally responded to my text messages, but only to let me know that she was *under the weather* and would be sending a girl named Beverly over to cover for her this week.

I found it unnerving that she already knew she would be out the entire week since we both knew she wasn't sick. She was avoiding me, and I hated it.

"Hey, kiddo, it's going to be dinnertime in a few minutes. Turn that down and go wash up."

He jumped around excitedly and then did as I asked.

Tonight's dinner was simple, just like it had been all week. I was too mentally exhausted to put more effort into cooking, and Alex wasn't a picky eater, so he didn't complain.

I pulled the meatloaf out of the oven, cursing when the door burned me as my hand slid past it. I tossed the pan onto the stove and set the towel by the sink as I ran cold water over the burn, trying to alleviate some of the pain. Sitting next to the sink on the counter was the Rudolph coffee mug that I'd bought Sunny, which hurt to look at more than the stupid burn. I missed her so much that I couldn't swallow past the emotions that rose up every single time I thought about her, which was probably why I hadn't bothered to put the damn cup away, forcing myself to be tormented by thoughts of her every time I saw it.

"You okay, daddy?"

"Yeah, Buddy, I'm okay. I burned myself, that's all."

I heard the chair scoot out, as I turned off the water.

"You ready to eat?" I asked, sitting down across from him and scooping some of the meatloaf onto his plate.

"Is mom coming?"

My hand froze midair as I worked the frustration in my jaw. It was the third night he'd asked for her after she told him she'd be back this week when she left on Sunday. I'd been playing along and pulling my phone out to "text" her, but I couldn't keep lying to him.

I set the spatula down and folded my hands in front of me on the table.

"I'm sorry, Buddy, but your mom isn't coming for dinner this week."

His face fell. I hated the sadness that washed over it.

"But she said she would."

"I know. And I'm so sorry that she said that. Your mom sometimes says stuff she doesn't mean and doesn't realize that it makes others sad when she doesn't follow through."

"Just like Sunny?"

My heart fell in my chest. I couldn't do this anymore. It was too much. He deserved so much better than this, but then again, he was only three and didn't need to know just how much people sucked. Not that Sunny sucked, but it sucked that she promised him she would be here this week and wasn't. That part definitely sucked, but I tried to put myself in her shoes and understand why she was avoiding us.

"Yes and no," I said gently. "Sunny hasn't been here this week because she's not feeling well. She'll be back when she's better." I felt uneasy saying that because I had no idea whether she'd be back or not at this point. I wasn't counting on it.

"Does she need to poop?"

I grinned, loving how that was always his go-to answer when people didn't feel well.

"Maybe. I don't know. But I know that your food will get cold if you don't start eating."

He smiled and then dug in. I tried to force myself to eat, but I didn't have much of an appetite these days. That was all out the window, along with my holiday joy, my zest for life, and my general ability to give a damn. And I had Sunny to blame for all of it.

By Friday, I still hadn't heard anything from Sunny. Beverly was doing well with Alex, but I had given her the day off since I'd officially closed the office early on

Thursday and given everyone Friday off since Christmas was on a Sunday this year.

I tried doing fun stuff and getting Alex in the mood to celebrate the holiday, but nothing I did worked. He didn't want to help me bake cookies. He didn't want to watch Christmas movies. He didn't even want to go to the park. I had never seen a child so sad before, and it broke my heart.

We stopped by Sugarplum Sweets for a treat when I ran out of ideas on how to make him feel better. Andi was working the register while Beverly helped with another cookie decorating class. She smiled and waved, offering us to join them, but I declined when I saw Alex's scowl.

"Maybe next time," I said as I headed to the register with him beside me.

"Hello," Andi greeted, smiling from me to Alex. "What can I get for you guys today?"

I looked down at him and nudged him with my arm.

"What would you like, Buddy?"

"Nothing." His arms were crossed over his chest as he continued to pout.

"Would you like a reindeer cookie?" Andi offered, leaning over the counter. "I just baked a fresh batch an hour ago."

"No, thank you."

She made a sad face at me and I felt like a failure for the tenth time today.

"Sorry, he's not having a good day. Can we get a dozen Christmas cookies to go?"

"Sure, not a problem."

She turned and grabbed a box from the counter behind her, then slid the glass and picked out an assortment of frosted sugar cookies that looked too good to eat.

A sharp pain shot through me as I remembered being here, decorating cookies with Sunny. Then it occurred to me that Alex was probably thinking about the same thing, which explained why his mood had soured so much once we got there.

"I know you miss her, Buddy," I said softly, rubbing his back.

"It doesn't matter."

He was angry, and I couldn't blame him. It'd been a shitty week for him, and we were two days from Christmas. What was there to be jolly about at this point?

"Anything else I can get you?" Andi asked, sliding the box across the counter to me.

"Do you have coffee?"

She scrunched her nose and shook her head.

"I do, but trust me, it's not as good as what you'll get from Sugarplum Latte. Sam's running a Christmas special today. You should stop by and check it out."

I looked at Alex, knowing he wouldn't want to go there and wait for me to order a drink.

"It's okay. I'll just take whatever you've got here. I think it's best if I get him home."

She looked down at him and smiled as she pulled her lips into a thin line.

"Let me get your drink, and then I'll have you on your way."

"Thanks."

I looked around the bakery, jealous of the families that were laughing and enjoying their time decorating cookies together. We had been that happy family a week ago, just the three of us. Right until Sharon came in and ruined everything.

A few minutes later, we were in the car and on our way home when I looked into the rearview mirror and saw my son. Without giving it any more thought, I took a sudden turn and headed to Sunny's house. One way or another, I was going to fix what was broken.

Twenty-Five
Sunny

I had just come out of the bathroom when I heard the doorbell. I glanced down at my reindeer pajamas and decided that I couldn't care less about appearances at this point. I'd finally gotten around to taking a shower this morning and brushed my teeth, but that was it. The PJs were in an effort to feel more in the Christmas spirit, though I had nothing to celebrate this year. There were presents wrapped and tucked under the small tree in the corner of my living room, but they were for Alex and Elliott, and I couldn't bring myself to go over there to give them to them.

The doorbell rang again, reminding me that someone was there.

I walked to the door and opened it, expecting Andi or one of my neighbors. Instead, Elliott stood there, looking over his shoulder to the driveway.

"What are you doing here?" I asked, colder than I intended.

He scrubbed a gloved hand down his face and exhaled heavily.

"I'm here to fix things. I know you don't want to see or talk to me, and that's fine. That's not why I'm here."

I crossed my arms over my chest, shielding myself from the cold air rushing in.

"Okay…"

"I need you to talk to Alex. I know that's asking a lot of you, Sunny, and I apologize. But I wouldn't be a good dad if I didn't try to do what's best for him. If you're not coming back, then I need *you* to be the one to tell him."

My head pulled back as anger started radiating through me.

"You're seriously going to use your kid against me?"

"No, Sunny. I'm not using my kid. I'm trying to fix his broken heart because this week has been hell on him, and damn if I haven't felt like I've failed him a million times since his mother walked through the door on Sunday. Nothing I say or do is working, and I'm lost, Sunny. For the first time in my fucking life, I'm struggling and don't know how to navigate this. I don't know how to keep from hurting him when people tell him they'll be there and then they don't show up. So yeah, call me an asshole if you want to, but I'm here because I'm asking for your help, and that takes a lot right now. But you know what, I love my son enough to do this for him."

I swallowed hard and looked past him to the SUV parked in my driveway.

"I don't like that you blindsided me with this, Elliott. You didn't give me any heads up and expect that I'm going to be able to talk to him without knowing what's going on."

"You haven't responded to me in almost a week. Why would I think that you'd listen if I called or gave you a heads-up? I'm doing my best here with the shit that's been thrown at us this week, but I can't keep going on like this. I can't stand to spend one more day with a depressed three-year-old, so I'm here to fix things."

I sucked in a cold breath of air and nodded to the driveway.

"Go get him and bring him in. I'll leave the door open while I go start some hot chocolate."

His face softened, and it looked like a load had been lifted off his shoulders as he took off to get Alex.

I went to the kitchen, grabbed a pot, and then began grabbing the stuff I needed for the hot chocolate. A few minutes later, I heard the door close. I looked up, expecting to see Alex come running to me, but he just stood there with a frown on his face, and his arms crossed over his chest.

My heart shattered into a million pieces as I abandoned everything and rushed over to him. I dropped to my knees and lifted his chin so he would look at me.

"Alex, I'm so sorry that you've had such a rough time this week," I said gently. I could feel Elliott watching me, but that didn't matter right now.

My concern was Alex and making sure to fix what I'd done.

"I know I promised to be there on Monday, and I'm so sorry that I had to break that promise. It wasn't anything that you did; I just wasn't feeling well and needed to stay home and rest."

His beautiful blue eyes finally looked up at me.

"Did you need to poop?"

I covered my mouth and burst out laughing. It felt so good to laugh, and I hadn't realized just how much I'd missed it.

"Yeah, I sure did."

"Are you feeling better now?"

I nodded.

"I'm feeling so much better. Thank you for coming to check on me."

I held out my arms and waited for him to be ready to hug me.

He rushed over and wrapped his arms around my neck as if he was afraid that I would disappear.

I stood and picked him up, holding him close to my heart.

"I've missed you so much, my sweet boy," I whispered, feeling the tears covering my eyes.

"I missed you too."

He pulled away and wiped my tears for me.

"Your dad said that you've had a hard time this week," I said softly, still holding him. "Do you want to talk about it over some hot chocolate?"

He grinned and nodded his head.

"Alright, I'll make some, and then we'll talk. In the meantime, how about we put some Christmas music on and dance?"

He clapped excitedly as I set him down and found the TV remote. I put on the Christmas music playlist that I had on Spotify and turned it up so he could hear it.

Everything felt like it had shifted again, and I couldn't

believe how much lighter I felt just from hugging him. He'd become such a huge part of my life that I couldn't stand the thought of being away from him.

Elliott followed me into the kitchen, which was technically the same room as the living room and only separated by a breakfast bar. I grabbed the ingredients I had set out and started the hot chocolate.

He leaned against the counter beside me and spoke quietly so only I could hear.

"Thank you for doing that," he said. "I can't begin to tell you how relieved I am to see him back to himself again."

"You don't need to thank me. I should be apologizing for putting him through that this week. I didn't mean to hurt him. I thought I was doing the right thing by staying away so he could bond with his mom."

"I haven't seen or heard from her since Sunday. Once I confirmed that I wouldn't give her any money, she disappeared."

"What?" I said, appalled that someone would do that. "But Alex was so happy to see her, and she seemed like she wanted to be there with him."

"She's a great actress. She should have gone to Hollywood and made a career out of it."

"So she just came back into his life and then left without any explanation?"

"It's what she does best," he said, gripping the counter behind him tighter. "When we got divorced, she asked for everything of value. The house. The car. The boat. She even asked for my dog, just to spite me. You know what I got?"

"What?" I turned to look at him while still keeping an eye on the hot chocolate.

"Full custody of my son. That's all I wanted."

"She didn't object to it or try for joint custody?"

He shook his head and looked past me to smile at Alex dancing to Jingle Bell Rock.

"She's never cared about being a mother. She left right after his first birthday and hasn't been back until the other day. She only cares about money and what she can get from me. I hate that he has a mother like that, but I can't change it. All I can do is manage who I allow into his life. When he's older, he can decide if he wants to have a relationship with her. But for now, I think he's better off without the constant disappointment of her not following through on the promises she makes."

"I'm sorry, Elliott; I had no idea it was that bad. I knew that you guys were divorced, but I really wanted things to be different when she came back. I grew up without a father because he died unexpectedly, so when I saw that Alex had another chance to have his mom in his life, I couldn't stand in the way of that. I knew how she felt about me, and I didn't want to be the reason that she didn't come around."

"I know, but Sunny, she would have done what she did whether you were in the picture or not. That's just who she is. She didn't even bring a single Christmas present with her for him. What kind of mom does that?"

"I can't imagine. I mean, I'm not his mom, but I have a whole stack of gifts under my tree for him," I laughed. "I love him, Elliott. More than I should, I know. But I do. I love him like he's mine, and that's been hard for me to process this week."

I felt the tears wetting the corners of my eyes again and hated that I was being such a crybaby this week.

Elliott reached behind me and turned off the stove before moving the pot from the heat. He stepped in front of me and wrapped his arms around my waist. I reached up and linked my hands behind his neck.

"I love how much you love him, Sunny. I didn't think I would ever find someone who would love my son as much as I do. But then you came into our lives and were like the piece of the puzzle we didn't know was missing until you were gone. We've both been miserable this week because you weren't there. I love you, Sunny. I love you so fucking much that it hurts not to have you. And Alex, he loves you like a mother. I'm not saying that you have to jump into that role, but—"

"Would you just shut up and kiss me?" I teased, lifting my lips to his.

His mouth eagerly sought out mine, both making up for lost time this week.

"Eeeewwww, gross!" Alex said from the living room

Elliott pulled away and rested his forehead against mine.

"Hey, Buddy, what do you think if Sunny was my girlfriend instead of your nanny?"

He came into the kitchen and looked up at us.

"Will she still play with me?"

"Yup. Everything will be the same, except I'll kiss her more often, and she'll probably spend the night with us more often."

"Can she live with us?"

I felt my heart flutter in my chest when I saw the way Elliott was looking at me now.

"I would love for her to live with us if she wants to."

"Does she still have to sleep on the couch? Or can she have her own room?"

Elliott made a scared face at me and then pulled away and looked at Alex.

"Well," he said nervously, bending down to be at eye level with him. "I was thinking that maybe she could stay in my room and sleep in my bed. Would that be okay with you?"

"Yeah, that's okay. Can we have hot chocolate now?"

I laughed, feeling more relaxed than I have in forever.

"Sure thing, let me grab some cups, and we'll go to the couch to drink it," I said, feeling Elliott's hand slip across my waist as he pulled me into him and kissed my neck.

Twenty-Six
Elliott

Sunny was the change that we all needed. After showing up at her house unexpectedly, I wasn't sure what was going to happen. I knew it was a risk because she was still upset about things, but I also knew that Alex needed to see her and talk to her. At the end of the day, it ended up being the best thing I'd ever done.

We spent the rest of the day at her house, playing games and laughing, all of the stress and bullshit from the week completely gone. By Saturday, we'd moved a handful of her things over to my house, including the gifts she'd bought for Alex and me. They barely fit under my tree after I brought out the gifts I'd bought for her and had been hiding until now.

That night we added the gifts from Santa after Alex went to sleep, and it looked like Christmas exploded in my living room. There were so many presents and yet there were only three of us. But what could I say? I loved every bit of it.

We ate the milk and cookies that Alex left out for Santa and then went to my room to catch up on the time we'd missed this past week.

Sunny was in the bathroom while I grabbed a few presents I had for her but couldn't have her open in front of Alex. When she came out, I was about to make a sarcastic comment about how long she was making me wait, then shut my mouth when I saw what she was wearing.

"Holy fucking reindeer balls," I muttered, looking her up and down as I licked my lips.

Her hair was pinned up, exposing her neck and showing off her cleavage in the red velvet bodysuit she was wearing with white fur trim. A tight red skirt wrapped around her hips and showed off her curves, but it was the fucking red and white striped stockings and stiletto heels that did me in.

"Merry Christmas," she said seductively, leaning against the doorframe.

"Merry Christmas indeed." I crossed the room in record time and picked her up, squeezing her ass as she squealed and giggled.

"I have gifts for you too, but they're going to have to wait until I'm done fucking you senseless."

"I have another gift for you, too," she said as I set her down on the bed.

She spread her legs, allowing the skirt to lift, and showed me the crotchless panties that were part of the bodysuit.

"Yes, yes. I accept your gift."

I crawled up the bed, ready to plant myself between her legs and devour my absolute most favorite treat in the world.

"Uh uh," she teased, shaking her finger at me. "Not yet."

I sat up and pouted, wondering why she was making me wait so long. Then she reached into the drawer of the nightstand and pulled out a wrapped gift that she handed to me.

While I was trying to focus on opening it, I caught a glimpse of her pulling the thin straps down her arms and then lowering the top of her bodysuit to her waist, leaving her breasts on full display.

I tore through the paper with far more aggression than needed, but I was hard as a rock and ready to fuck her.

She grinned and chewed her lower lip when I stared at the pack of double-stuffed Oreos in my hand.

I looked up at her and tilted my head, knowing there must be a reason she was giving me that look but not knowing why.

"Open them," she coaxed, nodding to the package I was gripping tightly in my hand.

"I think I'd rather eat you instead," I said with a shrug.

"Just open the damn cookies," she laughed.

"Okay, but yours is better."

I pulled the tab back and opened the package before extending it to her. After she took one, I got one and set the rest on the bed. I shoved it in my mouth and chewed quickly, ready to get on with the part I was excited about the most.

But Sunny took her time twisting the cookie and watching as she pulled it apart, leaving some cream on each side.

Then she took one and stuck it to her nipple before applying the other.

"What are you doing?"

"I thought you might want a real snack tonight."

She reached into the package and grabbed another one. My eyes stayed focused on her hands as she did the same thing, but this time, she took one end and reached down between her legs, rubbing it along her slit.

I was turned on beyond belief, but I also couldn't help but notice the crumbles that were coming off and making a mess on the bed.

"You okay?" she asked, a teasing tone in her voice.

"Mmmhmm."

"Having a hard time with the mess?"

I wanted to answer her and tell her yes, but when she parted her folds and slid the cookie between her lips, I couldn't get words out if I tried.

"Can I eat you out now?" I asked, the words strained in my throat.

She giggled and nodded as I pulled her down and licked my way up the inside of her thigh. I knew that there was cream getting mushed into the clean sheets I'd just put on this morning, but for once, I didn't care. Maybe messes weren't such a terrible thing if it meant I got to devour her pussy.

I looked up and watched her face as she propped herself up on her elbows to see what I was doing. She still had the cookies stuck to her nipples, but I would get to those in a second. I kissed the other side of her thigh and then made my way to her core, knowing how much it was driving her crazy that I was prolonging it.

One half of the Oreo was still sticking out between her lips, so I leaned in and took a bite, loving the way she gasped in response. Then I took another and kept eating until the rest was stuck inside of her. I used my tongue and swept it out, leaning up to let her watch as I ate the cookie that was wet from her arousal. Maybe I was into sweets after all.

Once I swallowed, I bent down and sucked her clit for a few minutes before she moaned and cried out my name as she came around my face.

I knew she needed a few minutes before she was ready for my cock, so I went to the bathroom and grabbed a warm wet washcloth to clean her up with, even though I had worked pretty hard to get all the cookie crumbs out with my tongue.

I laid beside her and stroked my cock as she watched, then leaned in and nipped one of the cookies off her nipple. I chewed quickly, eager to suck her nipples and get her off again. I handed her the other cookie and licked off the cream from that nipple before climbing over her and sliding inside.

She moaned as she took a bite of the cookie, and I couldn't tell if she was enjoying that or my thick cock inside her. When she tossed the rest of her cookie onto the bed and scratched my back, I had my answer.

Within minutes, I was pounding into her, fucking her with everything I had while she clung to me and rode out another orgasm. It was, indeed, the best Christmas Eve ever.

Epilogue
Sunny
Six Months Later

"Can you help me grab that?" I asked Alex, nodding to the rolling pin I'd dropped on the floor.

He laughed and chased after it as I waddled behind him.

"You're overdoing it," Elliott said as he walked up behind me and wrapped his arms around my waist.

"I'm just making dough for the pizzas," I assured him.

"And I told you I would help you when I was done with my meeting. You should have waited for me."

"Well, it's your fault I'm in this position to begin with." I laughed and turned to face him, my swollen stomach putting some distance between us.

"One of the best things I've ever done." He wiggled his eyebrows and rubbed a hand over my stomach. "Not only did you agree to marry me, but now you're carrying my babies."

"I know," I said happily. "Leave it to you not to do anything the easy way. Had to go and knock me up with twins."

"But I get to be a big brother," Alex said, bringing me the rolling pin.

"You're going to be the *best* big brother." I smiled and took it from him before handing it to Elliott.

"Alright, Buddy, how about you come help me get the pizzas going so Sunny can rest."

"Take it easy, mommy," he said, giving me the biggest grin.

I loved when he called me that. I hadn't asked him to, and neither Elliott nor I had talked about what we would do when we had the twins, but one day, he just started calling me Mommy on his own and we didn't correct him.

We hadn't seen or heard from Sharon since the day she showed up at Elliott's house. Alex was starting to understand more about his relationship with his mom and stopped asking when she was coming a few weeks after I moved in.

There was a lot of change, and we did our best to help guide him through it. Moving in was a big step for all of us, but I was surprised by how easy it was. It was also weird that I was engaged to Elliott but still *working* as Alex's nanny. I talked to Elliott about starting a daycare or doing something where I could still care for Alex but bring in my own income.

After a lot of back and forth, he assured me that he didn't want me to work because he'd rather that my focus stay on taking care of Alex until he went to school. Little did we know that I'd have newborns to take care of before that happened. While I didn't love the idea of not bringing in my own money, I felt better that I was still able to contribute around the house by cooking, cleaning, and taking care of Alex.

It was great having Elliott work from home, and we had even gone to the manufacturing plant a few times to check on some new products they were developing. After my new toys that Elliott gave me on Christmas Eve, I found that I couldn't get enough of trying new things with him. Toys were a regular part of our sex lives, and I was more than happy to be his little guinea pig when he needed to try out a new one.

I sat at the kitchen table and rested my feet on the chair across from me while watching my guys make dinner. They were laughing and telling silly jokes, trying to see who could come up with the best one. My heart felt as full as my stomach these days, and I wouldn't trade it for the world.

When I first agreed to be exclusive to Elliott as Alex's nanny, I never imagined it would go any further than that. Even though it was a great job, I gained something so much bigger than that—a family. And now, we were expanding it with two sweet girls on the way.

****

Thank you so much for reading Sunny and Elliott's story! If you're looking for more holiday romance, be sure to check out Blame It On The Mistletoe (Sugarplum Falls Book 1), or one of these other steamy novellas!

Blame It On The Mistletoe

https://books2read.com/u/bw1rqe

Snow Place To Go

https://books2read.com/u/4A560N

A Christmas Wish

https://books2read.com/u/4EKXpE

Holiday Hijinks

https://books2read.com/u/4DP6Ze

Chocolate Covered Mistletoe (Stone Creek Book 1)

https://books2read.com/u/3LRk9N

180

Other Books By Samantha Baca

The Haven Brook Series
(small-town romantic suspense):

'Til Death Do Us Part (Haven Brook Book 1)

https://books2read.com/u/m2RJNR

The Cradle Will Fall (Haven Brook Book 2)

https://books2read.com/u/b6O0QE

The Ties That Bind (Haven Brook Book 3)

https://books2read.com/u/mqgoz8

A Very Haven Christmas (Haven Brook Book 4- Novella)

https://books2read.com/u/mvqGjj

Three Strikes, You're Gone (Haven Brook Book 5)

https://books2read.com/u/mvqL2z

The Dark Shadows Series
(romantic suspense)

Five Steps Ahead (Dark Shadows Book 1)

https://books2read.com/u/38Q0gO

Ten Seconds Too Late (Dark Shadows Book 2)

https://books2read.com/u/3JRgVB

Against The Clock (Dark Shadows Book 3)

https://books2read.com/u/m2YwoR

Out Of Time (Dark Shadows Book 4)

https://books2read.com/u/4DKMoP

The Stone Creek Series
(small-town- novellas)

Chocolate Covered Mistletoe (Stone Creek Book 1)

https://books2read.com/u/3LRk9N

Candy Coated Promises (Stone Creek Book 2)

https://books2read.com/u/mldP5Y

Pumpkin Spiced Possibilities (Stone Creek Book 3)

https://books2read.com/u/bojdwV

Beaumont Creek Series
(small town)

Just One Time (Beaumont Creek Book 1)

https://books2read.com/u/3G52zK

Second Chances (Beaumont Creek Book 2)

https://books2read.com/u/4Aj6Z0

Third Time's The Charm (Beaumont Creek Book 3)

https://books2read.com/u/b5lEyG

Four-ever Single (Beaumont Creek Book 4)

Preorder link coming soon

Fifth Wheel (Beaumont Creek Book 5)

Preorder link coming soon

Whiskey Mountain Series
(small-town- novellas)

Something To Talk About

BLAME IT ON THE EGGNOG

https://books2read.com/u/4X62ag

Something To Think About

https://books2read.com/u/3GWAan

Something To Believe In

https://books2read.com/u/3yVzgB

Something To Live For

Preorder link coming soon

Sugarplum Falls Series (Holiday Novellas- can be read as standalone)

Blame It On The Mistletoe

https://books2read.com/u/bw1rqe

Blame It On The Eggnog

https://books2read.com/u/38PPY6

Standalone Books

One Last Wish

https://books2read.com/u/mqg7D9

Finding Love In Apartment 2C (novella)

https://books2read.com/u/bze9aZ

Cocky Counsel: A Hero Club Novel

https://books2read.com/u/31Kzkn

All Is Fair In Food And War (novella)

https://books2read.com/u/bp8qjX

Holiday Books (novellas)

Snow Place To Go

https://books2read.com/u/4A560N

A Christmas Wish

https://books2read.com/u/4EKXpE

Holiday Hijinks

https://books2read.com/u/4DP6Ze

Acknowledgements

Thank you so much for taking the time to ready this steamy holiday novella! I hope you enjoyed it!

I want to express my sincere gratitude to my editing team for tackling this one and making it the best book possible! Thank you Tillie! I appreciate all of my alpha and beta readers, especially the helpful feedback they provide along the way. Azucena, Chelsea, Claire, Amanda, and Kristen—I would be lost without you ladies. Thank you so much!

As always, I owe a lot to my family for their support and for providing me with the opportunities to write and get the words out that are constantly floating around in my head. I love you all so much and couldn't imagine not having you along with me on this beautiful journey.

My husband and girls are the greatest blessings I've ever been given and I hope I always make you guys proud. If I can do anything, I hope that I show you that it's possible to chase after your dreams, even when they feel big and scary.

To my ARC readers—thank you all for signing up for this one and for constantly spreading the love with my books! I simply adore you!

Thank you to the readers who continue to pick up my books and devour them. I see you (not literally because that would be super creepy!) and I appreciate you more than you'll ever know.

About the Author

Samantha lives in the southwest with her husband and two small children after abandoning her childhood dream of living in a cabin in Colorado when she found that she couldn't afford to live there and was deathly allergic to the woods. When she's not writing, she's usually spouting off sarcastic remarks while drinking wine out of a coffee mug to look like a functional adult while chasing down her toddlers. She enjoys spending time with her family, watching reruns of Friends, and the 24/7 flow of coffee that can be found in her veins. Be sure to follow her on social media for updates on what she's working on.

You can find her here:

Facebook: https://www.facebook.com/AuthorSamanthaBaca

Instagram: https://instagram.com/author_samantha_baca

Goodreads: http://www.goodreads.com/authorsamanthabaca

Facebook Reader Group:

https://www.facebook.com/groups/2945710968775398/

Webpage: https://authorsamanthabaca.wordpress.com

Newsletter: http://eepurl.com/g0NcSj